Blue Ribbon Romance

Virginia Smiley

BANTAM BOOKS

TORONTO · NEW YORK · LONDON · SYDNEY · AUCKLAND

RL 6, IL age 11 and up

BLUE RIBBON ROMANCE
A Bantam Book / January 1989

ISBN 0-553-27648-4

Published simultaneously in the United States and Canada

PRINTED IN THE UNITED STATES OF AMERICA

O   0 9 8 7 6 5 4 3 2 1

BLUE RIBBON ROMANCE

I walked to the doorway of the barn to see Troy standing, pitchfork in hand, in front of a wheelbarrow loaded with hay. His dark, wavy hair was rumpled, his jeans patched, and his shirt sleeves rolled high. Even from where I stood I could see his forehead was wet with perspiration. He looked as if he'd been transplanted to New York State from Texas or Wyoming. But in spite of the setting he looked terrific. My heart was thumping, but I tried to act natural.

"How about a cool drink?" I suggested.

His brown eyes looked into mine, unnerving me. I could feel a blush start to creep up my neck.

"Definitely," Troy declared. He reached out and took my hand, leading me toward the monstrous willow tree at the edge of the yard. "Come on, let's have a picnic over here."

My hand felt warm in Troy's grasp. I was afraid to move for fear that he would let go. *It's funny*, I thought as I tried to control my suddenly rapid heartbeat. *He's acting as if holding my hand is the most natural thing in the world. Does this mean he's beginning to like me as much as I like him?*

Bantam Sweet Dreams Romances
Ask your bookseller for the books you have missed

Blue Ribbon Romance

Chapter One

"**I** said I'll take care of it!" I exclaimed before taking a sip of freshly squeezed orange juice.

"You've been saying that for a month now, Ronnie," my dad reminded me. "When we agreed to take Gingersnap with us, it was under the condition that you'd find a stable to board her. A horse is fine in the open country of Indiana, but not in your grandmother's backyard in Honeyoye Falls."

He poured himself a second cup of coffee, while I stared into my bowl of cornflakes and tried to think of a reply. About a month ago now, my parents and I had moved to Honeyoye Falls, a small town near Rochester, New York. My parents had gotten new jobs in the area, and since my grandmother already had a big house here, we moved in with her. At first Mom and Dad had told me that we'd have to leave Ginger behind. Boy, was I ever miserable! Ginger and I had been the best of friends since I was a kid and she was a foal. I couldn't imagine life without her. Finally, Gram had come to the rescue by suggesting that I keep Ginger in the shed in her backyard. The yard is fenced in and there's a wide expanse of lawn. It was the perfect solution, except that we'd all agreed it was only temporary. I'd really have to find a permanent place for my horse—and soon!

"You know I'm very fond of Gingersnap myself," Dad went on, "but yesterday one of the neighbors phoned your grandmother. She insists she has more flies around her house this year."

I took a deep breath. Mrs. Axelrod no doubt. She was always complaining about something. "So maybe it's a bad year for flies," I grumbled.

My mother looked annoyed. She's plump and pretty, and when she smiles her blue eyes crinkle at the corners. At the moment, however, she had scowl lines on her forehead. I knew I was in trouble. "Ronnie, I don't see why you can't talk to your friend Lorie. She must know of a farm nearby where you can board Ginger."

I picked at a piece of toast, not really hungry. "I'll check into it today, I promise." The sound of a car tooting outside echoed in the kitchen. I gulped down the rest of my orange juice. "That must be Lorie now," I said.

Although I had only met her a month ago, Lorie and I were already good friends. From

2

my very first day at my new school, she had taken me under her wing, showing me the ropes and introducing me around. And now that her parents had bought a new car, giving Lorie full use of the old one, she was giving me rides to school as well.

I snatched up my books and headed for the door, briefly envying my new friend. I still had three months to go before I could apply for my driver's permit. It seemed like forever. "I'll see you later," I called over my shoulder.

Dad thumped his coffee mug on the table. "With good news, I hope," he said pointedly.

I sighed. Actually, I had told Lorie during lunch period last Wednesday that I needed a place for Ginger. She had immediately pointed out a boy sitting with friends at a table across the room. "That's Troy Bennett. He's a junior. His family owns Double B Riding Stables on the outskirts of town," she'd told me. "They give lessons there, and I think they board horses, too. He's cute, don't you think?" Lorie had sighed dreamily. "If I wasn't already hooked on Joe, I think I'd be *very* interested. It's too bad about his dad. He was in a car accident and now he's in a wheelchair. Troy has taken over a lot of the work at the stables. I can introduce you. . . ."

"Another time," I had told her. Up till then, I'd enjoyed meeting new people, but Troy looked unapproachable. I wanted time to think about what I'd say to him. Actually, for me, it was a classic case of "like" at first sight. He was around six feet tall, had dark wavy hair and dark brown eyes; and I could see by the way the other kids hung around him that he was popular. I really didn't want to mess up my first encounter with Troy Bennett. Since the day Lorie had pointed him out, I'd been mulling over what I'd say. I thought that after Lorie introduced us, I'd give him my best smile that showed off my dimples, and say, "Hi. I'm new in town. I understand your family owns a riding stable. I have a beautiful quarter horse mare named Gingersnap who needs a place to live. . . ." In my mind he smiled and said, "No problem, Ronnie. We have plenty of room."

Now it was more than a week later. I still hadn't mustered up enough courage to meet him. But today had to be the day. Gram's neighbors would complain about more than flies if Ginger didn't move out of the neighborhood soon.

Slipping into the passenger seat next to Lorie, I thought again about approaching Troy Bennett. I piled my books on the floor between my feet and pulled the safety belt across my lap.

Lorie watched me, shaking her blond head. "You look as if you've got something important on your mind," she remarked, putting the car in reverse and easing it out our long driveway. "Problems?"

Lorie was great. She was pretty, slim like me, and had a terrific sense of humor. And I was beginning to find that she had the uncanny gift of reading my mind.

"You could say that," I replied.

She laughed, turning the corner and heading the car toward the business district, where the few stores were starting to come alive for the day. "Let me guess. It concerns Gingersnap. Right?"

I nodded. "I have to get her out of Gram's shed before we're run out of town." I absently brushed my long brown hair over my shoulder. "Will you introduce me to Troy today?" I asked as casually as I could.

Lorie paused at a stop sign a few blocks from the school entrance and turned her amber eyes in my direction. "Sure, no problem. I told you I'd introduce you whenever you wanted to meet him. I see you're wearing your black jeans and a new sweater for the occasion."

Laughing lightly, she turned her attention back to the road. She parked in the school lot and we hurried inside to our lockers. Out of the corner of my eye, I noticed Troy working his combination a few lockers away from ours. My stomach started to turn somersaults. Luckily, the bell rang before Lorie noticed him, and we all scrambled for first period class.

Throughout math I thought about meeting Troy and rehearsed in my mind what I would say to him. I wasn't exactly sure what was making me so nervous. I guess it was just because he always looked so confident, so together. In a way, I wanted to meet him and get it over with, but then my stomach would turn a triple somersault, making me wish I could put it off a little longer.

I made it through my morning classes, and as always, Lorie met me at our table in the cafeteria. We opened our brown bags, comparing sandwiches with our friends Janet Turk and Margaret Chase. It was a daily ritual that had started on my first day when I'd brought chicken salad for lunch—Margaret's favorite. Since then we'd been trading sandwiches every lunch period.

"I'll give you my bologna for your tuna," Janet offered, looking at my thick sandwich with a longing expression on her freckled face.

"No way." Lorie snatched up half of my sandwich. "I get first choice today, remember. I'm trading with Ronnie." She handed me a gooey peanut butter and jelly sandwich, a move that increased the churning in the pit of my stomach. "Oh, no . . . you guys have to know one thing. Peanut butter makes me . . ." I covered my mouth and Lorie quickly

6

replaced my tuna sandwich and took back her own.

"So," Margaret giggled, "we've learned something else about Veronica . . ." I couldn't help smiling when she said my name, the way she rolled the *r* like a Scotsman. "Peanut butter is not her cup of tea. You know, if we were smart, we'd buy our lunch."

"And spoil our fun?" Janet shook her head. "No way."

The sound of male laughter behind us made Lorie turn her head. "Hey, there he is. There's Troy Bennett. Come on, Ronnie, let's catch him while he's sitting still." She jumped to her feet, reaching out to pull me after her. My first reaction was panic, but when I started to protest, Gingersnap's beautiful face flashed into my mind. She deserved a comfortable home. I squared my shoulders and followed Lorie to the next table where Troy was sitting with two of his friends.

His eyes were even darker and more intense up close. I couldn't help staring, and when Lorie spoke to him, I barely heard her words. He turned to smile at me. "Hello, Ronnie. What can I do for you?" His voice was deep and friendly.

I turned to glance at Lorie only to find she had retreated to our table. Suddenly I felt very much alone. I knew the warm sensation creeping up my neck was soon going to be a full-blown blush. I hesitated. What was it I'd rehearsed? "Lorie said you have stalls," I blurted out finally. It sounded dumb. I heard one of Troy's friends laugh. Taking a deep breath, I hastily added, "I'm looking for a place to board my mare."

Troy's dark eyes met mine. "You've come to the right place," he said, smiling straight at me. I wasn't sure if it was a friendly smile or one of amusement.

Troy motioned to the chair across the table from him. "Sit down, Ronnie, we can talk about it." He glared at his friends. "Don't let these jerks bother you. They're harmless, but they should be committed anyway. This is Jeff Marconi," he motioned to the husky black-haired boy, "and Marty Mills, sometimes known as Rusty."

"Hi," I mumbled.

"We'll get lost and let you two talk business," Rusty said, pushing back his chair.

I watched the two leave and move to a nearby table to talk with a group of girls. Behind me I could her my friends chattering loudly. But when Troy leaned across the table to talk to me the voices behind went silent, and I knew they were straining to hear what we were saying.

"So, you have a mare. What kind?" Troy seemed genuinely interested, and I felt some of my nervousness slipping away.

"She's a quarter, I've had her since I was eight," I explained. "We've done a lot of shows together. . . ."

"Hey, great. I ride in every show I can. I collect blue ribbons."

He said it in a matter-of-fact way, the way he might say, "I collect stamps."

He grinned at me. "How many have you won?"

For a brief moment I had the urge to lie, to say something to impress this terrific-looking boy seated across from me. Instead I shrugged. "I've won second and third . . . and fourth, but never first. I'm looking forward to that one."

He ran his fingers through his thick mane of hair. "Competition," he muttered. "Maybe I shouldn't rent you a stall. I might be sorry." A twinkle flashed in his eyes and I relaxed, knowing he was just teasing.

"Gingersnap needs a home . . . and *soon*," I said. "I've been keeping her in a shed in my grandmother's yard since we moved to town about a month ago. The neighbors are starting to complain."

He laughed. "I can imagine."

The bell rang, signaling the end of lunch. People around us snatched up their books and headed for the halls. I felt a pang of disappointment sweep over me. "About that stall . . ." I said.

Troy stood up, grabbing his stack of books. "Look, I have to run. If I'm late to trig Mr. Renaldi will skin me. Meet me in the parking lot after school, okay? If you like I'll drive you out to the farm so you can look around and see what you think of the place for your mare." Then he was gone, joining his friends at the door before I could utter a word.

My friends walked over to where I was standing and Margaret nudged me. "Hey, what were you two huddling about? Did you get a place for your horse?"

"Maybe. Troy is driving me out to see the farm after school," I announced. They exchanged wide-eyed glances.

"Lucky you. I've been hearing all kinds of things about Troy Bennett lately," Janet said suggestively. "He's quite a catch."

I rolled my eyes at her. "Janet, I'm not fishing. I just want a place to keep Ginger so I can ride again."

"Well, you can do that at the Double B for sure. Wait until you see it," Lorie exclaimed.

"Yeah." Margaret nodded, her jet black braid bouncing on her back. "I rode there once last summer. It's like a bit of the West right here in Honeyoye Falls. And Janet's right—consider the 'fringe benefits' if you board your mare out there."

I shook my head, laughing as Margaret arched her eyebrows in a comical way. "Come on, you guys, or we'll be late for gym class. I hate to make grand entrances."

I walked ahead of them, my head spinning with thoughts of the Double B—and Troy Bennett. I had to admit that the fringe benefits of boarding Ginger at the Double B were definitely on my mind. My stomach began churning again when I thought of waiting in the parking lot for Troy. What if he forgot? Maybe it was just something he'd said without thinking . . . something to end our conversation, like "See you later." It probably didn't mean anything at all. The parking lot was a big place. I'd feel like a jerk standing there alone waiting. Suddenly I wished I could skip the rest of the day—or at least look into a crystal ball and see how it would end.

Chapter Two

The rest of the afternoon dragged on and by the time the last bell rang I was almost a basket case. Lorie stayed by my side giving me moral support and advice.

"Stop worrying, you're only going to look at a barn after all. Troy will meet you, I guarantee it. He's a nice guy, Ronnie. Besides he's probably anxious to rent out a stall."

Her words didn't help. I took a deep breath and let it out slowly as we walked down the hall toward the door. "I should phone home to let them know where I'll be," I mused aloud. "Where I hope I'll be, anyway."

"Will anyone be home? I can stop by and fill them in if you want me to." Lorie reached over and took my books from my arms. "I'll drop these off for you. There's no sense carrying them to the farm."

I gave her a grateful smile. "Thanks. I owe you one." I clutched my shoulder bag nervously. "Mom should be home soon. She works

12

part-time at the insurance office on Main and usually gets home about the same time I do. Or if not, Gram will most likely be around."

"No problem," Lorie assured me as we walked out into the sunny parking lot.

After she left I stood facing the sea of cars, wishing the knot in the pit of my stomach would untie itself. "Why can't Gram own a farm," I muttered, hoping I didn't seem as nervous as I felt. I wasn't usually shy with boys. I'd had my share of dates back in Indy, but Troy seemed different somehow. The way he looked at me made my heart do flip-flops. I couldn't explain it to myself, and certainly not to Lorie or anyone else.

The parking lot cleared out quickly. I watched the cars turn onto the street and roar off down the road. Still I waited, feeling weird whenever a group walked past giving me those what's-she-waiting-for looks. I didn't know many of them so I didn't have to smile and make small talk.

I was sure Troy must have come out without my seeing him. He had probably gone on home already. It was a two-mile walk to Gram's but I figured I'd better hit the road. There were only a half dozen cars remaining in the student's lot now, and odds were that none belonged to Troy.

I walked toward the road, disappointment churning inside me. Well, that was that. Now

I'd have to find somewhere else to board Ginger. I recalled the twinkle in Troy's soft brown eyes and shook my head.

"Ronnie, you're a first-class jerk," I grumbled.

I didn't hear the car until it eased alongside me and a slightly familiar voice called, "Hey . . . I hope you hadn't given up on me. Come on, hop in." I turned to see Troy's face through the open window of the Honda Civic that I recognized as one of the six cars that had been left in the parking lot. "Old Willie kept a couple of us working on a project in science," he continued. "I didn't know how to contact you to let you know."

My heart beat a little faster as I climbed in beside him. "Nice car," I said, patting the plush blue velvet seat.

"She's not bad. It's my parents' car actually, but I can use it whenever I want to." He glanced at me. "Do you drive, Ronnie?"

I shook my head. "I will, though, in three more months."

"I bet you're looking forward to that," Troy remarked.

I grinned. "That's for sure."

We were both quiet then. I was trying to think of something fascinating to say, and Troy seemed to be concentrating on his driving. I gazed out the window at the passing scenery. I'd been through this part of town before, but I'd never paid much attention.

14

Now I noticed large clapboard houses separated by lots of lush green grass and trees. The streets were similar to those in my grandmother's neighborhood, but more open—in fact, the scenery kind of reminded me of Indiana.

At last Troy broke the silence. "So, tell me more about your mare," he said. "Is she a good show horse?"

"Ginger is terrific," I replied, thinking of Gingersnap prancing around the ring with her head held high. "I think it's me who needs the practice," I added. "What kind of horse do you ride?"

"A black and white pinto quarter horse I've had since he was a colt. Arrow and I have grown up together . . . and we both like to win." He smiled. "So consider yourself warned, Ronnie Wilson. Winning a blue ribbon around these parts won't be easy."

Troy's smile was friendly enough, but I detected an edge to his voice. "Well, I'm determined to start winning blues here, so watch out," I said with more confidence than I felt.

Easing the car onto a long dirt driveway, Troy announced, "This is it—the good old Double B. Mom and Dad started this farm when they were first married."

I stared at the large pastures on either side of the drive, each encircled by a white wooden fence. Several horses ambled close to the fence as Troy stopped the car. A black and white pinto at the far end of the pasture tossed his head, kicked up his heels, and galloped at full speed toward us.

"He's beautiful!" I exclaimed.

Troy jumped out of the car. "Come on . . . Arrow expects a sugar cube."

I followed him over to the fence as the pinto crowded past the other horses to the rail. Troy patted the horse's sleek neck before reaching into his pocket for a cube of sugar. "There you are, Arrow," he said quietly. "I didn't forget."

The horse neighed softly and nuzzled Troy's shoulder. I reached out to run my hand over the animal's soft muzzle. "Hello, Arrow," I murmured. "I'll bet you and Gingersnap will get along fine."

A chestnut mare stuck her head between Arrow and me and I patted her smooth neck, laughing at her pushiness. "Okay, you're gorgeous too."

"That's Pickles," Troy told me. "She's a boarder. So is Happy Wanderer." He reached out to stroke the nose of the Appaloosa standing quietly at the fence. "They belong to a doctor in town. He and his wife come out and ride on weekends." He gave Arrow another pat and returned to the car. "Come on, I'll show you the stables."

The stables were located at the end of

the drive near the house. I was impressed the moment we entered the larger barn. There were seven spacious box stalls on either side of the aisle and a door to the left opened into a large, neat tack room. The smell of leather tickled my nostrils when I went in to look at the saddles and other equipment. I noticed the bright colors on the wall and stared at the collection of blue ribbons.

"Wow!" I exclaimed, shaking my head in awe. "You really meant it when you said you like to win. I'm very impressed." That was an understatement. A glass case under the high window showed off several trophies of various sizes. On another wall a cluster of photos depicted horses and riders with brief notations underneath telling of their wins.

"Most of these pictures are of my dad when he was still riding," Troy said, coming up behind me. "He was in a car crash a few years ago that put him in a wheelchair. When that happened my mom gave up show riding too." He shrugged. "I do all of the riding for the family now."

The way he spoke and the sad look in his eyes tugged at my heart. "No wonder winning is so important to you," I said quietly. He gave me a puzzled look, and I quickly added, "Of course everyone wants to win. You know what I meant."

Embarrassed I turned to leave the room

and he followed. I wasn't much good at serious talk with someone I'd only just met. At the end of the barn we turned down a smaller wing and faced a towering mountain of hay bales and a large grain bin.

"You can see Gingersnap will eat well if she moves in with us," he said, suddenly laughing as he leaped onto one of the bales of hay. He bounded up one after another until he reached the top near the barn roof. "Come on up," he called to me.

I followed his lead and climbed up the hay bales, laughing as I stumbled over the top one and landed at Troy's feet. He reached down and pulled me up, and for a moment it seemed almost natural to have his hand in mine. Then, as if he had suddenly been burned, he pulled away and started back down the bales. "I'll show you where Gingersnap will be," he called over his shoulder.

It had only been a brief moment but a spark of magic passed between us. I had felt it, and I was sure Troy had felt it too.

Troy went back out into the bright sunshine and headed for the smaller barn, while I hurried to keep up with him. He paused at the door so suddenly that I almost bumped into him.

"Sorry," I said breathlessly.

He turned to look at me with an amused expression in his dark eyes. "I didn't realize I was going so fast," he said. "I guess there's just so much to show you."

He motioned me inside where more box stalls lined both sides of the barn. "Gingersnap would be in number one."

He stopped inside and opened the stall gate. Again I was impressed. It was large and clean, with a bin for hay and grain and a place for a bucket of water. There was a small window opening out to an outside paddock. I gazed around, taking it all in. "I like it. Gingersnap will think she's in horse heaven. When can I bring her out?"

"How about after school tomorrow? My dad and mom will be here then. You can meet them and talk over the fee."

The fee—in my relief at finding such a good home for Ginger, I'd almost forgotten about that. Ginger was worth any amount of money to me, but then I wasn't the one who would be paying the bills. I only hoped my parents were as fond of her as they claimed.

"We do it either of two ways," Troy went on. "You pay for the stall and feed and take care of exercise and grooming. Or you can pay for everything—feed, exercise . . . the works." He stepped from the stall into the aisle as I took one more look around, then followed, closing the gate behind me.

Troy had already moved on to the next stall, where a shiny black gelding poked his head over the gate, nudging Troy's shoulder. "This is Blackjack, he'll be Gingersnap's neighbor."

"He seems friendly," I remarked, reaching out to stroke the horse's mane. Blackjack lifted his head away from Troy and began licking my outstretched hand.

Troy and I laughed. "Blackjack sure is friendly—especially when he thinks you've got a treat for him," Troy said, sticking his hand in his pocket for another cube of sugar.

"He'll be a good neighbor for Gingersnap then," I said. I glanced at my watch. "I'd better get back home. Do you have a phone I can use? My mom should be home now and she can drive out to get me."

He shook his head. "No way. I drove you out, and I'll take you home. But before we go there's one more thing you should see." We walked back down to another wing of the barn. "What do you think of this? My dad built it himself."

We stood facing a huge indoor riding ring, very similar to the show ring back in Indiana. My mouth opened in surprise. "It's terrific!" I exclaimed. Now I'd be able to train anytime, rain or shine.

We went outside and walked toward his car.

A pickup truck pulled into the barnyard and squealed to a stop. Two young men hopped out, waving. "Hey, Troy, where are you going?"

"Just taking Ronnie home," Troy called back. "You guys saddle up. I'll be back in a few minutes."

"No problem," the taller one said. "We'll be out on the trails for an hour or so."

I felt guilty taking Troy away from the farm, but I was also glad he offered to drive me home. The time had gone by so quickly, and I had enjoyed every minute. I had a feeling things were going to be great. If all went well, the Double B would be like a second home, for I intended to be on hand every day if possible, to see Ginger—and also to see Troy.

Chapter Three

It didn't seem to take long to drive back to Gram's house. Perhaps that's because after only a few minutes of silence as we set out, we ended up talking the rest of the way home.

"Do you ride gymkhana?" Troy asked, referring to a type of competition that consists of fun games played on horseback.

"Let's say I'd like to," I replied. "I've worked with Gingersnap on a few of the basic games. We started with barrel racing last summer. An ex-rodeo rider lived near our place in Indiana, so he gave me a few lessons. How about you?"

He shrugged. "Still practicing. Arrow's good maneuvering the barrels, and I've tried him with pole bending, but he needs a lot of work before he can miss all the poles." Troy grinned. "Let's say we're no threat to anyone in the gymkhana class. . . yet."

"So, what do you ride?" I asked. It suddenly dawned on me that we wouldn't have to worry about competing against each other if we were interested in different events.

"Mostly Western Pleasure so far," he said, and my heart sank. "Arrow handles the three paces well. I might try trail class in one of the local shows this summer though. I think Arrow is ready." Troy steered the car onto Main Street, and past the insurance office where my mother worked. "What classes do you ride?" he asked.

I glanced away from him. "Western Pleasure," I answered.

"I guess we really are going to be rivals, then," Troy said quietly. "I was hoping we could avoid it somehow."

So he'd been thinking the same thing I had! Well, that was heartening anyway.

"Next left," I directed as we approached Gram's street.

Troy made the turn, smiling mischievously. "I guess this means you're going to win more red ribbons."

His voice was light, but again I detected an edge to it. If he could be so competitive, so could I. "Maybe you're the one who will have to get used to red ribbons," I said.

He laughed. "I doubt it."

I let his comment pass, but it strengthened my resolve to start winning blue ribbons instead of red. Troy Bennett would certainly be in for a few surprises!

I looked out the window again, just in time to see Gram's house up ahead. "That's our place on the right," I said, pointing to the big brick house. Troy pulled up next to the curb. "Thanks," I told him. "I appreciate you driving me out to your place and bringing me home. You've been a lifesaver, believe me. Gram's neighbor will be overjoyed when we move Gingersnap out tomorrow."

"Glad we had the empty stall." He checked his watch. "I'd ask to see your mare now, but I have a lesson to give in fifteen minutes, so I'd better get home." He turned to look at me, his fingers drumming the steering wheel. "Maybe we can train together for the horse shows," he said. "Having competition under the same roof will keep me on my toes. But I'm warning you, I'm out to win."

"So am I," I told him. "Anyway, you'd better not be late for your lesson."

"No way. I'm teaching a pretty redhead to ride," he said.

I didn't want to react to his words, but I did. "Lucky you," I told him sarcastically.

He grinned. "Dotty is the cutest eight-year-old I know. See you tomorrow."

"You're crazy," I yelled, watching him back out the driveway and turn onto the road before I hurried inside.

"Is that you, Ronnie?" Gram's voice called from the kitchen. "Lorie phoned . . . wants you to call her right away."

"Thanks, Gram," I called back, going into

the den to try Lorie's number. It made me feel good to come home and get a telephone message. Lorie's phone calls certainly made me feel that I'd been accepted in Honeyoye Falls. Now the busy signal droned in my ear, proof that she would be unavailable for at least an hour. She and Joe could really burn up the phone wires sometimes.

I ambled into the kitchen, following the delicious scent of homemade spaghetti sauce. "Mmm, it smells super, Gram." I sniffed the steam coming from the pot on the stove. "Lots of oregano." I turned to face her. "Guess what, Gram? Ginger has a home. She can move in tomorrow, and Mrs. Grump won't have to worry about swatting flies all summer."

Gram turned from the sink where she was filling a pan with water. She was sixty-one but she looked more like forty-one. Her skin was nearly smooth and her hair had only a sprinkle of gray. Her gray eyes twinkled behind her gold-rimmed glasses. "So you finally met the Bennett boy. It wasn't so bad, was it?" She put the pan of water on the stove.

I reached into the cupboard for the dinner plates and started to set the table. But my mind was on Troy. "Now you're teasing, Gram. I told you I'd talk to him. I just wanted to wait a couple of weeks to meet him so I didn't seem pushy. Now I can see I should have talked with Troy sooner. He's really very nice."

"Of course he is. All the Bennetts are nice." Gram spread a loaf of Italian bread with butter and sprinkled the top with garlic powder before slipping it under the broiler.

"I'm curious, Gram. Why didn't you get in touch with them before we moved in to see if they could board Gingersnap?" I asked.

"I could have spoken to them," Gram admitted. "But I thought it was up to you to arrange for Gingersnap's keep." She stirred the spaghetti sauce as she spoke. "I took care of Lance Bennett after his auto accident. In fact, I lived at the farm for a few weeks until he was able to get around in the wheelchair. I'm surprised Troy didn't tell you."

I stared at her. Gram is a practical nurse, but I didn't think she had taken on any live-in cases in the last few years.

I started setting out the napkins and flatware around the table. "We didn't talk much, just about the stall and things like that. I'll find out more tomorrow when I take Gingersnap out to the farm." I paused for a moment, watching Gram at the stove. "What's Mr. Bennett like?"

"Lance Bennett? He's a fine man who was given a bad break. He isn't able to ride now, or do much of the work around the stables, but he keeps the books, takes care of the tack, things like that. He's adjusting well. He does have one rather big problem though.

For Troy's sake I hope he can work it out."
Gram's forehead creased in a troubled frown.
I was about to question her when Mom came
in carrying a couple of bags of groceries. I
took one of the bags from her and set it on
the counter.

"Thanks, Ronnie." Mom's voice was breathless. "I was lucky. I stopped at the supermar-
ket later than I intended and ran into this
handsome man at the meat counter. He offered to help with my groceries."

I pretended shock. "Mom. . . at your age.
What will Dad say?"

Just then my father came into the room
carrying an armload of grocery bags. His dark
mustache wiggled when he smiled. "He'll say
he shouldn't have stopped to see if the mar-
ket had any good steaks."

I laughed. Mom and Dad were the greatest.
While Mom was small and pretty, Dad was
tall, dark, and rugged looking. They were still
happy after almost twenty years of marriage.
I hoped I would be as lucky some day.

Mom and Dad were pleased that I had talked
to Troy and found a home for Gingersnap.
They even told me not to worry about the
cost.

"Ginger is one of the family," Mom said.
"I'm glad you found a place so nearby."

"That's right," Dad agreed. "I know I've been
nagging you lately, but that's because I didn't

want us to be forced to get rid of her. I'm glad it's worked out. In fact, I'll even take you and Ginger over to the Double B tomorrow afternoon."

"That would be great. Thanks, Dad!" I replied. "I'm going to run outside and tell Gingersnap the news."

"Dinner in five minutes," Gram called after me as I grabbed a carrot from one of the grocery bags and ran out the back door.

I had just enough time to explain to Ginger that she'd soon be moving to the Double B. I know it seems absurd to think that she understood, but honestly, I think she did, and she seemed happy.

After dinner I went up to my room to try Lorie's number again. This time she answered, sounding breathless.

"It's about time you called," she exclaimed. "I've been anxious to hear about what happened at the Bennett stables. How did it go? Was Troy friendly? Do you like him? Are you going to board Gingersnap out there?"

I giggled into the phone. "Simmer down and I'll tell you. I *did* try to call you. You know the result."

"Okay. I admit Joe and I talked for a while. So . . . how did it go?"

"Fine. I love the Double B. It's a fabulous stable. Dad and I are going to load Gingersnap into the trailer and take her out there tomorrow after school. Dad said he'd get out of work early so we can get her settled." I paused, knowing what would come next.

"Go on . . ." Lorie urged. "What else?"

"Sorry there isn't anything more exciting to report. That's it." I could almost see her disappointment. I think she expected instant romance. "I just finished supper. Now I'm going out to saddle Gingersnap and take a ride around the trails near the woods. Then I suppose I'll have to do some homework. And after a while I'll go to sleep," I said flippantly.

Lorie growled into the phone. "You're being a pain. I don't care if you ride to Buffalo. I want to know about Troy." She paused, then continued. "I checked around and found out he isn't seeing anyone special now," she continued after a pause. "He keeps so busy at the farm he doesn't have time for dates. Being out there every day maybe you can change that."

I twirled the phone cord. "Lorie, you're a hopeless romantic. Troy is very nice. He's quiet and friendly and polite. He even insisted on driving me home, which was sweet of him. What more can I say? I'm not interested in a romance," I lied. "I just want a place to ride and keep Gingersnap. I intend to get in a lot of practice and enter every local horse show this summer."

"I *know* that," Lorie replied in exasperation. "By the way, I found out something you should know from one of Troy's friends. His father *really* wants him to win. I guess before his car accident Mr. Bennett used to ride in shows and always brought home blue ribbons. Now he expects Troy to do the same."

"Thanks for the warning," I told her. "I gathered that this afternoon. I'll just have to work harder, that's all."

It was great riding in the cool May air. The breeze blew my hair straight back and made my cheeks tingle. Gingersnap was especially frisky, enjoying her first long ride in a week. I didn't try to control her. Instead I let her run as hard and as long as she wanted on the deserted trail. I felt free, as if I were in another world, and Gingersnap seemed to feel the same way.

At last we turned around to ride back home. Ginger took a while to cool down, and it was late by the time I put her in the shed for the night. Inside the house, my parents and Gram were watching a movie on TV. It must have been exciting because they barely noticed me pass through the living room on my way upstairs to shower before finishing my math homework.

When I finally went to bed I couldn't sleep. I turned on my side and stared at the white ruffled curtains fluttering as the warm breeze tugged at them. I wondered about Mr. Bennett. Was Lorie's warning what Gram had meant about a problem, I wondered? Was Mr. Bennett living through Troy now that he could no longer ride himself? I felt sorry for Troy. It must be tough to always feel the pressure to win. My parents only ever want me to do my best. But still, I felt sorry for Troy's father. It must be terrible to love to ride and suddenly not to be able to . . . ever.

I sighed. Perhaps I was making a big deal out of nothing. Only time would tell what would happen. I was sure of one thing, though—it promised to be an exciting summer. I flipped over onto my back to stare up at the high ceiling. My thoughts drifted to the following day, and I finally fell asleep wondering how Gingersnap would react to her first glimpse of her new home—and whether Troy would be around.

Chapter Four

At school the next day time seemed to drag. I'm not usually a clock watcher but I glanced at the clock on the wall every time the hands clicked. English was the last period of the day, and by then I was especially restless. We were reading *Hamlet,* and for a treat our teacher Mrs. Chambers had brought in a video-cassette of the film starring Sir Laurence Olivier. Unfortunately, I barely saw it. My mind was on moving Gingersnap to her new home. The second the bell rang I snatched up my books and joined Lorie in the hall.

"I've got to get right home," I told her, letting my eyes search the crowded hall for a glimpse of Troy. I hadn't seen him all day and wondered if he would remember that I was bringing Gingersnap to the farm this afternoon. "I don't want to miss the bus."

Lorie hurried to keep up with me as we wove in and out to pass the stragglers. "Too bad I had to leave the car at the garage this morning," she said. "The motor was knocking and Dad thought it should be checked. Wouldn't you know Joe couldn't get his father's car today! I hate buses," she remarked with a snort. "Hey, there's Troy up ahead with Pete Lang."

I followed Lorie's gaze, and sure enough, there was Troy at the other end of the hall with another boy. I deliberately slowed my steps. I don't know why, but seeing Troy leaning against the wall talking to his friend made my nerves jump into action. Should I say something or just pretend I didn't notice him? I sighed. I was really acting dumb. Troy wasn't a stranger, and I'd be seeing a lot of him from now on.

We were almost in front of them when Troy glanced up. For a brief instant I thought he was going to turn away. Then recognition lit up his face and he flashed an infectious smile in our direction. "Hi, you two," he greeted us. "Is Gingersnap ready for her move?"

I returned his smile, nodding. "Dad and I will bring her out in a little while."

"Are you girls catching the bus?" he asked, noticing the way I glanced toward the door where the buses were parked outside.

Lorie gave a deep, morose sigh. "Yeah I don't have the car today. Wouldn't you know, just when Ronnie wants to get home early."

I wanted to strangle her. I could feel the color creep up my neck and flood my face. Troy just shrugged, though, not seeming to notice that I looked like a ripe tomato.

"Hey, no problem. I can give you girls a lift." He turned to his friend. "Pete, why don't you and the other guys meet me at the Double B in about an hour for a trail ride, okay?"

Pete nodded. "Will do."

"Then my chariot awaits," Troy said with a mock bow. "This way, girls." Troy lead the way to the door.

Lorie fell into step beside Troy so I did the same. He's probably just being friendly since I'll be boarding my horse at his parents' farm, I told myself. So why was I so jittery?

Lorie kept up a steady conversation in the car, so luckily I only had to listen. I was amazed at the way she could keep talking and not run out of things to say. She went from sports to teachers to summer vacation without a pause.

Once he let Lorie off at her house, Troy turned the car radio on to a popular music station, so I didn't have to say much then either. I still couldn't understand why I was so nervous with Troy, when only the day before I'd felt that I'd taken a major step in getting to know him.

"I'll probably see you later at the farm if you stick around a while," he said as he pulled up outside Gram's house. "I have to give a lesson to a know-it-all tomboy. She's eleven, and I think she expects to win big money in the rodeos by the time she's twelve." His laugh was hearty. "Then I have the trail ride with the guys; but after that I'll be around. I couldn't miss mucking out the stalls, could I?"

I laughed self-consciously.

"We have a guy who works for us, but I help when I can," he went on. "It's a lot of work for one person."

I nodded. "I can imagine. It's enough work with just one horse to care for." I slid out, clutching my books so I wouldn't drop them. "Thanks again, Troy. I appreciate the ride. I'll probably see you later," I added quickly, shutting the car door. As I headed up the walk to the front steps, I knew he was watching. I could feel his eyes on my back and it unnerved me. At last I heard the motor start and a light toot of the horn as Troy drove away.

When I went inside Dad was already there, making himself a giant Dagwood sandwich in the kitchen.

"The car is in the back," he said. "I've already hitched the trailer, so all we have to do is pack Gingersnap's tack, then we can take off any time you want."

"Is Mom coming along?" I asked, stacking my books on the table.

"She phoned to say that she's working late tonight at the office," Dad replied. He sliced his sandwich in half. "What a masterpiece. Do you want me to make one for you while you pack the tack?"

My stomach rumbled in response. "Okay," I agreed. "Just a quick bite though. I'm anxious to get Gingersnap settled in at the farm."

When we drove into the farmyard an hour later, Troy's father was seated outside in his wheelchair, busily rubbing saddle soap into a hand-tooled saddle on a table in front of him. When he heard the car he looked up from his work and wheeled over to greet us. I was surprised at how much Troy looked like his father. When Mr. Bennett smiled, his brown eyes crinkled at the corners just like Troy's. He extended his sun-bronzed hand to Dad. "You must be Mr. Wilson." He looked up at me and offered his hand. "And Ronnie. Troy told me to expect you." He wheeled to the back of the trailer where Gingersnap's red tail hung down over the gate, switching like a plume. "So this is our new boarder?"

"I've told her all about her new stall," I said, heading for the trailer to open the gate. I talked quietly to Gingersnap, reassuring her that everything was fine before I unhitched her and backed her out of the trailer. Ginger was used to riding to shows, so she wasn't the least bit skittish. She just whinnied softly when we were on solid ground and nudged my shoulder.

Mr. Bennett came up beside her and reached up to pat her shiny back. "Nice mare," he said. "Good lines. I'll bet she's a winner."

"She's done well when Ronnie has shown her," Dad told him.

I walked Gingersnap around in a circle to limber her up and let the two men talk. I wanted to show Gingersnap the corral and the barns before leading her into her stall. The other horses noticed the new arrival and came over to the fence to greet her. Only one laid back his ears and snorted. "Oh, no. You're supposed to be neighbors," I told the black gelding. "Now be nice."

Gingersnap whinnied. Blackjack answered, his ears perking up. "That's better," I said, laughing.

Mr. Bennett and Dad went into the barn office to discuss costs while I led Gingersnap to her stall. Fresh straw covered the floor, and the bin was full of hay. Gingersnap sniffed at it a moment before munching the meal in front of her. I patted her silky neck and watched her silently. She was at home. For the first time since we'd moved to Honeyoye Falls I felt completely relaxed. Now I could concentrate on training Gingersnap for the first summer horse show. My spirits soared. I had the feeling this was going to be the year I won my first blue ribbon. . . whether Troy liked it or not.

I am so glad it's Friday, I thought as I gave Gingersnap one last scratch behind her ear. That meant that I could spend all weekend riding. I left Ginger, already content in her new home, and went out to meet Dad. The air was a bit cooler now, and the sun was sliding down behind the trees that bordered the corral, painting the sky with bright orange streaks.

As Dad and I walked to the car, I heard the sound of horses' hooves coming from the trail. A moment later Troy and his friends rode into the barnyard. I saw Troy gesture to his friends, then ride over in our direction. I liked how Troy sat tall in the saddle, a lock of hair poking out from under the brim of the cowboy hat he wore shoved back on his head. My heart went into double time looking at him.

"Hi," I greeted him shyly, returning his smile. "How was your ride?"

Troy watched his friends dismount and unsaddle their mounts. "Not bad. We covered about six miles. The fresh air really wakes you up after a long day behind a desk." His grin widened. "I see you've moved Gingersnap into her new home. I'll take good care of her for you."

"Thanks, Troy. Oh. . . this is my dad. Dad, meet Troy Bennett."

"Good to meet you, sir." Troy extended his hand.

Dad reached out to shake Troy's hand. "I've heard a lot about you and the Double B. From what I've seen here today I think Gingersnap is in good hands." He glanced at his watch. "We'd better be on our way now, Ronnie. I left a note saying we'd be home by seven, and it's already past that."

I nodded and headed toward the car.

"I'll be here early tomorrow to ride," I told Troy. "I want to get busy working with Gingersnap."

Troy hopped off Arrow's back. "See you then," he said as he led the horse toward his friends, who were already cooling down their mounts.

I got into the car and watched through the window as Troy removed Arrow's tooled saddle. By the comfortable way he behaved around the horses, it was obvious he had been working with them a long time. Gingersnap would be in good hands. When Dad started the car I settled back to relax.

We drove home more quickly unhampered by the trailer. Mr. Bennett had said we could leave it behind the barn with the other trailers and Dad had thought that was a great idea.

"I'm quite impressed with the Bennetts' stables, Ronnie," Dad said as he turned out of their long driveway. "The inside riding ring will be great in bad weather. You'll be able to work out with Gingersnap even if it's pouring rain." He chuckled. "Although knowing you, you probably wouldn't care as long as you're in the saddle."

"Very funny, Dad," I said with a grin. "Actually, I'm going to need a lot of practice if I'm going to win any blue ribbons. From what I hear, Troy will be hard to beat."

"But he hasn't ridden against Ronnie Wilson yet. From what I hear, she's pretty good, too," Dad teased.

"Thanks for the vote of confidence, Dad," I said. "I'll do my best to win."

Suddenly his voice was serious. "Ronnie, you know we'd love to see you win a blue, but remember that winning isn't the most important thing, okay?"

I nodded absentmindedly, imagining how my room would look with a wall covered with blue ribbons like the Bennetts' tack room.

As soon as I entered the house I hurried to the phone to call Lorie. I knew she'd want to be filled in on Gingersnap's move, and for once her line wasn't busy. As I settled back in Gram's easy chair to wait for Lorie to answer the phone, I looked out the back window. A strange, sad feeling swept over me when I saw the empty hay-strewn shed and the grass in the big backyard cropped short from Gingersnap's grazing. Suddenly my stomach felt achy and weak. I was glad to have a good home for Gingersnap, but already I missed seeing the shiny red mare right outside the window.

"Did you get Gingersnap moved to the Double B?" she asked after saying a quick hello. "Do you think she likes her new home? Did you see Troy? Did you—"

"Hold on a sec," I said. "Give me a chance. Yes, we moved Ginger to the Double B. Yes, she seems happy at the stables. And I only saw Troy briefly. Anything else?"

Lorie laughed. "My mother just told me I'm too nosy. I don't think so. I'm just interested in my friend's well-being. Right?"

"Sure." I saw Gingersnap's old halter hanging on the fence and stared at it. Tears started to fill my eyes and I brushed them away.

Lorie cleared her throat. "Anything wrong, Ronnie? I hear quiet on the other end of the line."

I swallowed hard. "No, I'm fine," I said.

"Well, you don't sound fine."

I sighed, wiping another tear from the corner of my eye. "I think I know how a mother feels when she sends her child off to school for the first time. I miss Ginger already. Back in Indiana, we had a barn right on our property for her. This is the first time she's ever been away from home."

"But, Ronnie, you'll see her every day . . . and Troy, too, you lucky girl." She giggled into the phone. "I wish I had a horse to board at the Double B."

I laughed. Lorie had a way of boosting my spirits. I was lucky to have found such a good friend in Honeyoye Falls. Just then Gram called from the kitchen, asking me to help her and Mom frost brownies for the bake sale the PTA was holding in the morning. "I have to go, Lorie. I'll see you tomorrow."

After we hung up I stared out the window for a few moments before I headed for the kitchen. My mind would not be on the baking, I was sure, but I tried to put my moments of gloom behind me. Gingersnap was in good hands.

Chapter Five

Saturday dawned clear and warm, a perfect day for riding. I dressed in my old faded jeans, boots, and my new red V-necked cotton sweater with a red, blue, and green plaid shirt underneath. Then I pulled my hair back into a French braid before dashing downstairs to breakfast. Dad and Gram had already gone to the school to set up for the bake sale. Mom sat at the table making out checks for the monthly bills and sipping a cup of coffee.

"There's cinnamon toast," she told me as I hurried into the kitchen. "I like your hair like that, Ronnie."

"Thanks. Margaret does hers like this." I picked up a slice of crisp toast and munched it, pouring orange juice to wash it down. It didn't look like a good time to bother Mom, but I did anyway. "Can you drive me to the farm, Mom? I want to spend the day with Gingersnap, and see how she's getting on at the Double B. We're going to need a lot of work to get ready for the first show too. School will be out in two weeks and Troy said there are always quite a few shows after that."

"Do you think you'll be ready by then?" Mom asked.

"I'm sure going to try," I told her. "How about it, Mom . . . could you please drive me to the stables? I'll give you my first blue ribbon."

Mom finished writing a check, put it in the envelope and stood up from her chair. "I'm ready for a break from bills." She laughed and streched her arms over her head. "And I'm not due for my shift at the bake sale for a while, so let's go."

I went to the refrigerator for a carrot, stuck it into my back pocket, and followed Mom out the back door.

When Mom let me off at the Double B, I immediately hurried into the barn to greet Gingersnap. At the sound of my voice I expected her beautiful head to appear so I could rub her velvety muzzle before handing her the carrot. But the stall stood empty, with clean straw covering the floor. I felt a pang of disappointment.

"She's in the corral," a familiar voice called from the doorway of a stall farther along in the barn.

I turned to see Troy standing, pitchfork in hand, in front of a wheelbarrow loaded with manure. In spite of the setting he looked terrific. His hair was rumpled, his jeans patched, and his shirt sleeves rolled high. Even from where I stood I could see his forehead was wet with perspiration. He looked as if he'd been transplanted to New York State from Texas or Wyoming. My heart was thumping, but I tried to act natural.

"Did I actually catch you *working*?" I teased, pretending surprise.

"I do a lot of that," he answered, turning back to his work. "I turned Gingersnap out a while ago."

"I think I'll take her out on the track for a while and put her through her paces," I told him. "I hope she remembers all of her tricks."

Troy straightened, leaning on the fork. Now it was his turn to feign surprise. "Are you saying we're boarding a talented horse here at the Double B?"

I nodded. "Sure thing. Didn't I tell you? Ginger can count to ten, stretch, and rear on cue. I trained her myself."

"You'll have to run her through her tricks so I can see them," Troy said. "I'll be out to ride after I finish cleaning out the stalls. Maybe we can practice together."

His dark eyes looked into mine, unnerving me. I could feel the color start to creep up my neck and I turned toward the tack room. "I'd better get Ginger saddled up," I said. "See you later."

"Heck . . . I thought you'd at least offer to help me out," he called as I left the barn.

"No way," I said with a laugh. "That's what I'm paying you for."

"I'm crushed," he shouted after me. "I'll get even on the track later. Arrow isn't going to be beat by the new horse in town."

"We'll see," I yelled over my shoulder. "You know where to find us."

Gingersnap was across the field grazing with several other horses. I whistled lightly and she raised her head, neighing in reply. When she saw me at the fence she trotted over, tossing her beautiful head and snorting a greeting. I put the saddle on the ground while I went to the corral gate to bring Gingersnap outside. She nudged my shoulder, whinnying softly until I pulled the carrot out of my pocket.

"I didn't forget," I said, rubbing her velvety muzzle. "Here's your treat." She crunched the carrot, then pawed the ground. "You are a spoiled rotten horse," I said, laughing. Her head turned and she nibbled at my back pocket. "Okay, Okay. Of course I have sugar. . . ." I fed her two cubes. Satisfied, she stood quietly while I put on the pad, saddle blanket, and saddle, then tightened the cinch around her belly and slipped the bridle over her head.

Gingersnap was lifting her hooves restlessly now, impatient to go for a ride.

As soon as I had mounted, we rode to the training ring where I put her through the basics—walking, trotting, and cantering. Then we started on her special tricks. Gingersnap was in the middle of her limping act when Troy rode Arrow into the ring.

"Did she pick up a stone?" he asked in a concerned voice.

I laughed and trotted her around in a circle. "I told you she's well trained. That's one of her tricks."

Troy pushed his hat back on his head, grinning. "She sure had me fooled. How is she at maneuvering the barrels?"

"She can hold her own," I told him.

"I'll set up a few and we'll see how she does. Arrow usually wins in the junior rodeos I've entered him in." He glanced at me. "Worried?"

I patted Gingersnap's silky neck. "No way. Just set out those barrels and I'll show you." Gingersnap pawed the ground, eager to be off and running.

As soon as the barrels were in place Troy made a running leap over Arrow's rump into the saddle. *Show off!* I thought. Actually, I was impressed but I didn't intend to tell Troy. I was sure he knew he was good.

I watched him ride around the ring, warming up before he let Arrow attempt the barrel race. He was an excellent rider, and when he began to maneuver Arrow in between the barrels, I realized why he had won so many blue ribbons. Never mind, I told myself. I certainly wasn't going to give up so easily. Having the competition where I could see him could be a big advantage.

It was my turn now. I took a deep breath and squeezed my legs around Ginger's sides. That was all the prompting she needed. She took off so fast, I thought for sure she'd sideswipe a barrel, but she knew exactly what to do. When we'd finished Ginger had tied Arrow's time.

Troy pulled up beside me, shaking his head. "You're not bad . . . neither is the mare."

We tried again and again, with Arrow beating us three out of five times. After the last race I felt breathless and alive. Perspiration trickled down my forehead.

"That's what I call a good workout." Troy mopped his brow with his kerchief before dismounting. "The best I've had in a long time."

"Me too," I agreed.

We walked the horses a while to cool them down before turning them into the corral. When we turned away from the fence Troy pointed to the driveway. "Hey, there's Lorie."

Lorie stopped her car and hopped out as Joe Burke climbed out from the other side.

"Hi," she called, waving us over. "Your mom said you'd be here, Ronnie, but I kind of figured you would anyway. We brought a treat—picnic for four, how's that?"

Joe's red hair gleamed like a new penny in the noonday sun. He held up a picnic basket. "That's right. We brought along the entire kitchen. Except for the sink and stove," he kidded Lorie. He gave Troy and me a warm smile.

"And some leftover desserts care of the PTA bake sale," Lorie added, ignoring his ribbing. "You two look like you need something to perk you up."

"You couldn't be more right," I moaned, rubbing the seat of my pants. "I am tired and *sore*. We've done some hard riding. You two are a pair of angels. I can't think of anything nicer than sitting down with a cool drink."

"Definitely," Troy declared. He reached out and took my hand, leading me toward the monstrous willow tree at the edge of the yard. "Come on, let's have the picnic over here."

My hand felt warm in Troy's grasp. I was afraid to move it for fear that he would let go. *It's funny,* I thought as I tried to control my suddenly rapid heartbeat. *The other day when Troy took my hand to pull me up the hay bales, he had dropped it like a hot potato after only a brief moment. But now he's acting as if holding my hand is the most natural thing in the world. Does this mean he's beginning to like me as much as I like him?* I sneaked a glance up at Troy's face just as we reached the willow tree.

"Right here, everyone," he said. "This is a good spot." Then he dropped my hand to help Joe spread out the picnic blanket.

I sighed. My imagination had been running in high gear again. Most probably Troy only thought of me as a fellow horse freak who just happened to be a girl.

Lorie's voice brought me back to the present with a jolt. "So, is everyone ready for finals next week?" she asked, opening a bag of chips.

I groaned. "Bite your tongue, Lorie. We don't want to talk about school on a day like this."

"She's right," Troy agreed, handing me a can of soda. "I can't wait for vacation to begin. I want to enter as many shows as I can."

"I hear Wellington Stables in Mendon is putting on a show in a couple of weeks." Joe tossed his sandwich wrapper into an empty bag and reached for the bag of chips. "I have a cousin out that way and she rides at Wellington every year. I guess it's some sort of charity affair."

Troy nodded. "I'll be there."

I took a long swig of soda and reached into the basket for a sandwich. "Count me in. Where do I sign up?"

Troy drained his bottle of cola and leaned back against the willow tree trunk. "I have the phone number inside. I'll give it to you later so you can sign up." He winked at me. "You're going to have to do some fancy riding to get Gingersnap in shape."

I wrinkled my nose at him. "What do you mean 'get her in shape'? Gingersnap is ready right now. We just let you win before because we didn't want to hurt your male ego," I teased.

"No fighting, guys," Lorie proclaimed, brandishing a pickle in front of us.

I broke up giggling.

"Okay, okay," Troy agreed good-naturedly. "But you just wait for the Wellington show," he warned me.

There was contented silence while everyone was busy munching on fruit and cookies. "Do you want a ride home, Ronnie?" Lorie asked after a while. "We go right past your house, so it would be no trouble to drop you off."

I shook my head emphatically, my braid bouncing on my back. "I plan to get back in the saddle. I have a lot of riding to do today. Thanks anyway. I'll just phone home when I need a ride."

"You don't have to do that," Troy said. I looked at him in surprise. "I'll take you home later."

Before I had a chance to thank him, we heard a voice coming from the direction of the house. "It's good to see you kids enjoying the shade from this old tree," Mr. Bennett remarked as he rolled his wheelchair toward us.

"It's a terrific spot for a picnic," I told him.

"It certainly is," he agreed, reaching for a chocolate chip cookie from the collection of bake sale leftovers. Troy quickly passed the plate to his father.

Smiling, Mr. Bennett took a cookie. "We used to have lots of picnics here when you were younger, Troy. Remember? Then we'd hop back on our mounts and race back to the corral."

Troy looked pleased. "Sure, I remember, Dad. In fact, I'll be back in the saddle in a few minutes. Maybe you could give me a few pointers."

Mr. Bennett took another cookie from the plate that Lorie passed around. "Let me know when you want me. I'll be in the tack room. I noticed that tooled saddle needs a good soaping," he said, taking an extra cookie before wheeling around for the stables.

Watching Troy and his father, I could understand Troy's desire to win blue ribbons. His father seemed so strong and vital, I could just imagine him getting up from his wheelchair and hopping on a horse. But of course that was one thing he simply couldn't do. It was so sad. I admired Troy for the way he included his father in his training.

With a sigh, I scrambled to my feet. "Well, I've rested long enough. Thanks for the picnic, you two. How about hanging around to watch us work out in the ring?"

Lorie and Joe exchanged glances.

"I don't think so," Joe replied, "but thanks anyway."

We all bent down to clear up the remains of our picnic from the ground. As I reached over to pick up a stray napkin, Lorie gestured to me.

"How's it going?" she whispered as I knelt down next to her.

I knew exactly what she was talking about, but pretended I didn't. "What do you mean?" I whispered back.

"How's it going with Troy?" she hissed. "He held your hand before. That's definitely a good sign."

I shrugged as if I wasn't concerned, but I couldn't fool Lorie.

She waited a moment, then said aloud, "Hey, Joe and I are going to the movies tonight. *Super Aliens* is playing in Henrietta. Why don't you two come along?"

Troy looked at me and my heart beat doubletime. "How about it, Ronnie? Are you ready for *Super Aliens*?"

I laughed. "I can take it if you can." That was an understatement. I was ecstatic! I caught Lorie's eye and gave her a grateful smile. A double date with Troy! Lorie was a genius.

Chapter Six

Troy and I rode all afternoon, practicing the events we would face in the Wellington show. Gingersnap and Arrow were about evenly matched. In fact, if I had been judging their performances I wouldn't have been able to call a winner. Both horses were energetic and had the same rhythmic stride when we walked them, going as fast as they could without breaking into a run. I had found after years of riding Gingersnap that she responded best when I let the reins go slack and simply squeezed my legs against her sides.

Mr. Bennett sat close to the ring to watch us work out, and now and then he nodded approval. When Troy tried to back Arrow in a straight line and horse balked, Mr. Bennett called out, "Use the rein. . . ."

Troy nodded. I watched him use his rein lightly to urge Arrow straight backward, then to either side. I knew Gingersnap and I couldn't do as well. We both needed more work on the reverse. But Mr. Bennett motioned for me to give it a try and Troy sat back in his saddle to watch, so I couldn't refuse. My stomach knotted when I pulled back on the reins.

"Come on, Ginger," I whispered. "You can do it."

She backed up slowly, going off to the right. I knew immediately I had given her the wrong signal.

"A little more practice and you'll have it," Troy told me. "It isn't as easy as it looks."

That was certainly true, but I wanted Gingersnap and me to be good at all the events in the Western Pleasure class. I made up my mind we would practice reining back until we were perfect.

Troy and I worked long and hard in the ring until we were exhausted and Gingersnap and Arrow were ready for a rubdown.

Mr. Bennett watched us quietly as we groomed our horses. When we had finished he smiled his approval. "Young lady, you're quite a worker," he said.

"Thank you," I replied with a smile. "I've been taking care of Gingersnap for a long time. My dad says it isn't work for me, it's a labor of love. I guess he's right."

Mr. Bennett nodded. I wanted him to say I rode well, or he liked the way I sat in the saddle, but he didn't mention our practice session.

On the ride home, however, Troy and I talked nonstop about the afternoon's practice and the upcoming show. I felt so comfortable talking to Troy as long as we kept to the subject of horses. Even when he showed his competitive streak, I felt I could hold my own. After all, the real test would be at the show in two weeks, and by then I'd make sure I was ready.

But when Troy stopped the car in Gram's driveway, the easy conversation suddenly came to a halt.

"So, uh, I guess I'll see you tonight," I said.

Troy tapped the steering wheel. "Yeah, I'll pick you up at seven-thirty. Okay?"

"That sounds good," I agreed. I hesitated, feeling I should say something else, then just climbed out of the car. "See you."

As soon as I got inside, I rushed to the telephone to call the number Troy had given me, and in five minutes I was signed up for the Wellington show.

Then humming my own made-up, out of key tune, I showered and changed into my new denim skirt and royal blue soft-knit sweater that Gram had given me on my last birthday. I brushed my hair, letting it hang full and loose past my shoulders, and touched my lips with rose-pink gloss. By the time Troy pulled into the driveway again, I was ready to dash out the door.

"That's what I call being prompt." He gave me his biggest smile as I slid in beside him. "You look great."

I checked out his yellow sweater. "So do you."

Lorie and Joe were waiting for us in the lobby of the cinema in Henrietta. The movie was just starting so we quickly bought a bucket of popcorn to share among the four of us, and sat down in the back row. We munched the salty popcorn and laughed at the crazy antics of the scaly, ten-foot aliens from a planet called Ozonia. The movie definitely didn't tax our brains, but it was great just being there with Troy's arm around the back of my seat. Every now and then he moved and I could feel his arm touch my neck.

Sometime about halfway through the movie, he moved his arm down and took my hand in his. I leaned back, thinking how lucky I was. A week ago Troy had been a stranger and now . . . I didn't want tonight to ever end. But of course the Ozonians finally had to say their garbled goodbyes to the Planet Earth and blast off for home in their gold-plated spaceship.

With the Super Alien problem solved and the theater lights turned up, the four of us walked out into the cool spring night.

"Let's go across the street to the Pizza Cave," Joe suggested. "All that action made me hungry."

The Cave is a dark little place, but we discovered they serve the thickest, gooiest pizzas we had ever tasted. Madonna's latest hit blared from a flashy jukebox in the corner of the room and a few couples danced in a small area near the back.

When Joe finished his pizza he pulled Lorie to her feet. "Let's show them how it's done."

Troy and I watched them in silence for a few minutes, then he shrugged and asked, "Do you want to dance, Ronnie?"

I had an idea he didn't want to dance so I shook my head. "Not really. I have two left feet," I said with an apologetic smile.

He looked relieved. "Thank goodness. I have two rights."

"We could cause a disaster out there on the dance floor." I laughed. "We'd better stick to horseback riding. The world will be a little safer."

I don't think I ever enjoyed an evening as much in my life, and I hated to say goodnight when Troy dropped me off at the house a short time later.

He turned to face me in the darkness of the car. "Will you be out to the farm tomorrow?"

I nodded. "Sure thing. I'll have to leave early

tomorrow afternoon though. Exams start next week, so I'd better hit the books and study."

"Don't remind me of unpleasant things." He leaned so close I could smell his musky aftershave. My heart thumped wildly. Troy Bennett was about to kiss me! I moved closer to meet him halfway. When our lips met, it was in a light, tender kiss. Then he quickly pulled away.

"Tonight was great." His voice was husky.

I nodded, whispering, "I think so too, Troy."

Silence filled the car and I reached to open my door. "I'd better get inside before someone turns on the porch light to remind me what time it is."

Troy restarted the car. "I'll see you tomorrow, Ronnie. Good night."

I stood beside the porch steps until his car vanished around the corner. A sudden breeze tugged at my hair and caressed my face. Sighing, I went up the steps and into the house, my fingers touching my lips where he had kissed me. I knew that as long as I lived I would never forget this night.

The heavens opened wide on Sunday, deluging the area with heavy rain. And my throat had the scratchy feeling that signals the beginning of a cold. When Gram heard my croaky voice at breakfast she went into her "I'm a nurse" routine, taking my temperature and forcing a second glass of orange juice on me. Mom turned mother hen and hovered over me. Between the two I felt like an invalid.

"I'm fine," I assured them.

"You're staying in today," Mom said firmly. "Being new in school you can't afford to miss exams next week."

Groaning, I gulped down more orange juice. "If I drink any more juice there's going to be a tidal wave in my stomach."

"Fluids are good for you," Gram said.

I knew it wouldn't do me any good to argue with either of them. Dad had retreated to his basement workshop and was not going to be any help at all. He might have suggested that I go to the farm and ride Gingersnap in the indoor ring. Actually it would have been fun . . . and cozy. Just me and Troy working our horses and listening to the rain on the tin roof. I decided to give it another try.

"But I *have* to ride today," I told Mom and Gram. "I'm entering the Wellington show in three weeks. You know Gingersnap hasn't been worked out much lately."

Two heads shook in unison. "You phone Troy and tell him you aren't feeling well. Maybe he'll offer to exercise Gingersnap for you today." Mom's tone sounded final.

I scowled at the mound of scrambled eggs on my plate. "Gingersnap won't like that," I sputtered.

Mom's forehead wrinkled. "You're staying in and that's that. You're running a temperature. This weather could send you into pneumonia."

"Mom!" I was exasperated. "Ninety-eight point nine is *not* what I'd call a temperature. I'm not a child—"

The ringing of the phone brought the discussion to an end. When Gram handed it to me shaking her head, I knew it was Troy.

His tone was one of gloom. "I'm afraid I won't have much time for riding today. Mike—the guy who works for us—just called in sick. So I've got to muck out the stalls, exercise the horses, groom them—everything on my own. It's bound to take most of the day. Sorry about that."

"I can't go to the farm anyway," I said. "The two Wilson doctors have grounded me."

"Are you okay?" He sounded concerned.

"Just a dumb cold," I told him. "Nothing will keep me away from the stables after school tomorrow. I've only got an English exam, then I'm through for the day. How about you?"

"I have a science exam in the morning and algebra after lunch. I should be home early . . . two or so. I'll see you then." There was a long pause before he added, "Ronnie, I really did have a great time last night. I hope we can do it again sometime."

He hung up before I could reply, but his

words were the tonic I needed. I smiled brightly at Gram and Mom sipping their coffee at the kitchen table. "You two are absolutely right. I'll rest today and fight off this bug." I headed for the living room. "I'll be on the couch."

I caught the smile that passed between Mom and Gram. They obviously thought they had won.

Chapter Seven

The following morning the rain was still falling in torrents. My cold was bordering on the full-blown variety—runny nose, watery eyes, and itchy throat, but there was no way I could stay home. I had to go to school and face my English exam. Not that I was afraid I would flunk, as English was my best subject. I just wasn't in the mood to take a test.

Luckily, Lorie had the car so we didn't have to stand outside in the rain waiting for the bus. She arrived at the house gloomier than the weather, which was unusual for Lorie. I noticed her mood the second I climbed into the car.

She glanced my way, wrinkling her nose. "You look terrible."

"Thanks . . . you don't look so great yourself," I said. "I have a cold, what's your excuse?"

She backed the car out of the driveway and

headed toward the school. "After you left us Saturday night Joe and I went to the Ice Cream Palace, right? Well, who should saunter in but that Babs Turner. She slithered right over to our table, then she proceded to gush all over Joe. And"—she pounded the palm of her hand against the steering wheel angrily—"he gushed back. It was sickening. He actually acted as if he was thrilled to see her. You know how she is . . . sticky—like Elmer's glue."

I nodded. "Stickier." I didn't know Babs very well, but she was in my history class and was always flirting with the boys.

"All the guys love her act," Lorie continued. "Well, I stood it as long as I could, then I told Joe goodbye and left. I figured he'd come after me and leave Babsy sitting there, but he didn't." She drew in a long breath. "I haven't heard a word from him since. Well"—she tossed her head—"who cares?"

We pulled into the school parking lot and she found an empty space. "Obviously you do," I told her. "Look, I'm no expert on love, but don't you think you overreacted just a bit? I mean, Joe didn't ask Babs to join you, did he?"

She shook her head.

"That should tell you something. You're the one who walked out. For what it's worth, I think you should make the first move." I pulled my purse strap over my shoulder and got out of the car.

Lorie didn't mention Joe again, but I had the feeling she was considering my advice. She looked deep in thought when we walked into school.

As we approached our lockers, I saw Troy and his friends standing ahead in the hall, leaning against the wall outside the science room. I had the urge to turn down another hall, but I wanted to dump some of my books in my locker. I definitely wasn't at my best. My nose looked like an overripe cherry from so much blowing and my eyes were puffy. I was a mess.

When Troy spotted us, he left his friends and came over to say hello. "Hi, Lorie. Hi, Ronnie. I missed seeing you yesterday." His dark eyes appraised my face and he shook his head. "I thought you said you only had a dumb cold. Are you okay? You don't look very good."

I knew he was only showing concern, but my cold had made me touchy. "I'm fine, thank you," I snapped.

He grinned at me, reaching out to touch my arm. "Hey, calm down. You look good to me anyway . . . red nose and all." I glanced behind Troy where Lorie was rolling her eyes and pretending she was playing a violin. "Are you still going to be able to come to the farm today?" he went on, oblivious to Lorie's antics. "We can ride inside. Dad said he'd set up a few jumps."

Behind Troy, Lorie nodded her head vigorously. Of course I wanted to go to the Double B, but at that moment, I just didn't feel up to it.

I shrugged. "I'll see how I feel. I'll probably be there."

"There isn't much time to get ready for the Wellington show," he reminded me.

What does he mean by that remark? I wondered. *Is he implying that Gingersnap and I need a lot of practice?* "You worry about your own riding," I told him, my anger rising.

Lorie moved past Troy, her face serious now. "Come on, Ronnie. We want to get to English and relax a few minutes before the exam starts. Let's go. See you around, Troy."

She gave me a pointed look, and I suddenly realized how foolish I'd been acting. I felt a pang of guilt at the way I had snapped at Troy. "Good luck with science," I told him, sniffling when I smiled. "I'll see you at the stables."

He winked at me. "Take care of that cold." He rejoined his friends near the science room door, calling as an afterthought, "Good luck in your exam too, Ronnie. And I hope you feel better by this afternoon."

I walked faster to catch up with Lorie. He *did* care, I thought, my spirits rising. His last words had brightened the cloudy morning.

The exam was a breeze. I finished early, and so did Lorie. She suggested we stop at Burger Barn for a quick lunch, then she'd drive me out to the Double B. I called Mom at work from the school office and filled her in on my plans, assuring her my cold was much better and I'd be riding inside.

"If I can't get a ride home I'll call you or Dad . . . have a good day," I told her before I hung up.

The clouds were breaking up, and patches of dark blue were peeking through when Lorie turned the car down the long drive to the Double B. The color of the sky reminded me of the blue ribbon that I was determined to win. *You've got a lot of work ahead of you, Ronnie Wilson,* I told myself. *But you can do it.*

I rode Gingersnap easy at first. A couple of people were riding outside, but I was the only rider using the indoor ring. It was kind of eerie being there alone with just Gingersnap's whinnies, the saddle's creaking, and the soft sound of the mare's hooves on the earth to break the silence. I was glad that I could see the daylight streaming through the skylights in the ceiling. It made riding there alone a little less spooky. Soon, however, I became so engrossed in my practice that the surroundings didn't matter.

I didn't even notice when the door opened and Mr. Bennett wheeled his chair into the little viewing room at the end of the barn. Gingersnap saw him first, her ears pricking up as we passed the window. It was then that I glanced over, to see Troy's father watching me intently. He raised his hand in a wave. I smiled at him and continued around the ring, urging Gingersnap into a lazy lope, her favorite gait. She responded to my touch, breaking into a gallop, then after twice around the ring I slowed her to a trot and finally to a walk. Each time she responded quickly to the touch of my knees. Still, I had the feeling Mr. Bennett was finding fault with every move Gingersnap and I made.

When Troy entered the ring on Arrow I felt relieved—that is, until Mr. Bennett started booming out his comments through the microphone in the viewing room. Troy rode around the ring a few times, using different gaits the same as I had.

"Troy, you're not tight enough on the reins. The horse won't know what to do unless you tell it." Mr. Bennett called out to him in a gruff voice.

Immediately I noticed Troy tense up, clenching his hands around the leather reins. But Arrow didn't like that at all, and protested by snorting loudly and jerking his head from side to side.

"Not that tight," Mr. Bennett snapped.

I couldn't understand Mr. Bennett's problem. From my position in the ring I felt I had a better view, and I certainly hadn't seen anything wrong with the way Troy had gripped the reins in the first place. But I knew I'd better keep my mouth shut. Troy looked embarrassed enough as it was, and I didn't want to make the situation worse.

Troy and I kept riding, and Mr. Bennett kept finding different points on which to fault his son. Troy listened without objection, but I could see the tension in his face.

I was glad Dad would never tell me what to do in the ring. He was a good rider too—that's where I'd gotten my love for horses—but after teaching me to ride, he'd left me on my own. "I'll be here if you want advice, but I won't hover over you," he'd told me. And I liked it that way. We both enjoyed our occasional rides together, but I never felt like he was trying to run the show. But then I thought about Mr. Bennett and tried to imagine what it would be like to be confined to a wheelchair, not to be able to ride when horses meant everything to you. I don't think I could bear to just sit and watch others. I could almost understand why Mr. Bennett acted as he did.

His voice was quiet when it broke into my thoughts. "You won't get a blue ribbon by resting on your laurels, Troy."

"You're right, Dad," Troy said wearily as he reined Arrow around.

"Why don't you keep up until suppertime?" Mr. Bennett said in a kinder voice.

Troy nodded and walked Arrow alongside Gingersnap. "If you don't mind waiting, we can stop off at the Burger Barn before I take you home," he suggested. "Deal?"

I smiled. Of course I could wait! I didn't even care that I'd already been to the Burger Barn for lunch. "Deal," I agreed.

I rode a while longer, trying a few jumps and a barrel race, during which Mr. Bennett shouted a constant stream of instructions to Troy. When he shouted, "You can beat her . . ." I decided to give up for the day. It would be hard enough to compete against Troy without his father adding to the tension. I'd been riding for over an hour longer than Troy anyway, so I decided to groom Gingersnap, then call home and check in with my parents about my plans while I was waiting for Troy to finish his practice session. I had an idea his father was glad to see me leave the ring, although he did call over the speaker, "Nice riding, Ronnie. You've got a good horse there."

I waved my thanks and led Gingersnap out of the barn.

At the Burger Barn, we ran into Lorie and Joe on their way in. They were holding hands and smiling at each other, their argument obviously forgotten.

"Hi, you guys," I greeted them. "Funny meeting you here."

Lorie laughed. "Yeah, wasn't it just this afternoon we had lunch here?"

"You had lunch here?" Troy echoed, giving me a curious look. "Why didn't you tell me? We could have gone somewhere else."

"That's okay," I assured him. "I love Burger Barn burgers. Honest."

Troy shrugged. "Whatever you say."

"Now that that's settled, why don't Troy and I get the food, and you two find a table?" Joe suggested. "The lines are getting longer and I'm hungry."

"Good idea," Lorie said.

We quickly gave the boys our orders, then

Lorie dragged me off in search of a table. It only took a few minutes for her eagle eyes to spot a family getting up from a table in the corner. We rushed to grab it.

"So tell me what's going on with you and Troy," she demanded the minute we sat down. "Things must be going well if he's taking you out to dinner."

"I don't know what's going on," I replied. "He just asked if I wanted to stop off at the Burger Barn on the way home. I don't think that means anything."

"Of course it does, Ronnie!" she exclaimed, leaning forward in her seat. "He obviously likes you."

"Do you think so?"

"Ronnie, open your eyes. He drives you home from the stables all the time. He practices with you for the horse shows even though you're determined to beat him," Lorie said. "Now that's what I call deep like."

Lorie's words were encouraging, but I wasn't that sure of myself to believe her. I knew my feelings for Troy were growing stronger all the time, and I didn't want to be disappointed.

"I've only really known him a few days," I said at last.

Lorie rolled her eyes in frustration. "So? Joe and I knew the day we met that we were destined to be together."

I couldn't help giggling. "Except when Babs Turner gets in the way."

"That was nothing," Lorie scoffed. "I overreacted."

"Don't you think you're overreacting now?" I asked. "I think Troy just likes me as a friend."

Lorie sighed. "Have more faith in yourself. Listen, in the five whole weeks we've been friends, have I ever steered you wrong?" I shook my head. "And I'm right about this. Believe me, I know what I'm talking about."

"You know what you're talking about?" came a voice from behind. "Hah, that's a first," Joe teased, appearing with a tray of burgers and fries.

Troy followed close behind with another tray. "What are you talking about?" he asked, a puzzled look on his face. He set the tray on the table and scooted into the booth next to me.

I immediately felt a blush rising in my cheeks and glanced at Lorie for an answer, but this time she didn't have a quick reply.

"Oh, um, we weren't talking about anything really," she stammered. "Just girl talk, you know."

The heat in my cheeks intensified. Of course he knew what she meant by "girl talk"! Now Troy was sure to realize that we'd been talking about him. I pretended to be fascinated by the sesame seeds on my burger bun.

74

"Want to let us in on it?" Joe asked.

"No," Lorie answered abruptly, shoving a French fry in his mouth. "So, how did you do on your science exam, Troy?"

"I think I did okay, but there were a few questions that really had me stuck," he said. "How was the English exam?"

I sighed in relief and began to enjoy my dinner as the talk turned to school and exams and plans for the summer. I only hoped that Troy's plans included making me more than just a friend.

Chapter Eight

The remainder of that week and the next were a hazy blur. Summer vacation was about to become a reality and excitement ran high. Exams ended. My cold became ancient history. The whole world looked rosy and I had the feeling that the coming months would be perfect.

On the afternoon of the last day of school, we all cleaned out our lockers and stood around talking. Margaret kept looking at her watch.

"I have a job interview at the drug store," she told us. "If I'm going to go to Yale in a couple of years I have to start saving up."

"Yale?" My mouth dropped open. "Last month you were going to Cornell."

"Next month it will be Oswego. That's where Jimmy Townes plans to go." Janet opened her locker for one last look inside. "I guess this is it. Let's get together often this summer. Okay?"

"If we aren't all working," Lorie grumbled. "My parents want me to get a job this summer too."

"Hey, don't be so gloomy, you guys," I said. "This is the last day of school. We're supposed to be happy, remember? I'm sure no matter what we're doing this summer, we'll be able to get together now and then." I looked at the three girls who had welcomed me into their group. "I've only just gotten to know you. I'm not going to lose you now."

"Ronnie's right. Come on," Lorie cried, slamming her locker shut. She raced down the hall with the rest of us following until we finally ended up in the bright sunshine outside. Then Lorie whirled each of us around in turn. "We're free!" she whooped.

"What a feeling—no more homework!" shouted Margaret.

"No more school for three whole months!" Janet added.

"Happy summer, everybody!" I yelled, falling to the ground with dizziness and laughter.

Troy and I were getting along well too. We spent a lot of time together, especially now that school was over for the year. On most days I would ride alone until Troy finished his chores, then he would join me in the ring. There was always something to keep him busy when he wasn't in the saddle, but I never heard him complain.

I never heard him complain about his father's harsh remarks either, despite Mr. Bennett's continued criticism of his performance during our practice sessions in the ring. As for me, I could see marked improvement in both of us, and although we rarely entered into direct competitions during our practices anymore, it was obvious that we were well matched.

I refused to let my feelings for Troy get in the way of my determination to win a blue ribbon, though. For the most part, I succeeded by thinking of him as two separate people: there was Troy Bennett, the boy who made my heart do flip-flops whenever he smiled at me, and Troy Bennett, a stranger who would be my main rival at the horse show.

In the evenings we'd sometimes go out with Lorie and Joe, and Troy proved that he, too, could forget about the pressures of competition. The four of us usually spent most of the time teasing each other and laughing, and Lorie would do her best to encourage the romance between Troy and me. To her it was simple logic that since she and Joe were a couple, sooner or later Troy and I would pair up as well. But so far it seemed as if we were just good friends.

"It's only a matter of time," Lorie said more than once. "You like him, and I'm sure he likes you."

I sure hoped she was right.

The following week, on the day before the Wellington show, I helped Troy groom the horses. Neither Troy nor I talked much as we worked. I guess we were both keyed up—I know I was. When Troy drove me home soon after we'd finished, the tension in the car hung like a heavy fog. I hated it, but I wasn't sure what to do about it. Lately my stomach had begun to feel achy whenever I thought of the horse show, now more than ever. I started to get out of the car but Troy put his hand on my arm, giving me one of his super smiles.

"We're sure a bundle of laughs today, aren't we?" His infectious smile cleared the gloom from the car. "I guess I get kind of quiet and moody before a show. I hope you understand."

I nodded. I was always a nervous wreck before a show, but this time it was worse. Tomorrow I'd be competing against Troy. "I feel as if a hive of bees has taken up residence in the pit of my stomach," I told him. "And I guess I'm a little scared. I don't want things to change between us. Let's make a promise. There won't be any hard feelings if one of us wins a ribbon, okay?"

"It's a deal." He reached over to turn my face toward him. "See you tomorrow, Ronnie," he murmured, letting his lips touch mine in a feather-soft kiss.

That night I lay in my bed thinking of Troy, the show, and red, yellow, and blue ribbons until I finally drifted off to sleep.

The weather cooperated for the Wellington show. It was a warm, super sunny day. I dressed in my best jeans with a red Western-style shirt and red belt, and I'd even polished my riding boots for the occasion. When I looked at my image in the full-length mirror in the upstairs hall I was satisfied. I looked like a winner even if I didn't exactly ooze confidence.

Gram had fixed an early breakfast but my stomach churned too much for pancakes. I toasted an English muffin and managed to eat half and drink a glass of orange juice. I wouldn't have even eaten that if Mom hadn't insisted.

"Stay calm," she told me. "I know you're going to do just fine today."

"Of course she will," Dad said, diving into his stack of pancakes.

Gram poured herself a cup of coffee. "We'll all be there to root for you and Gingersnap. Just—"

"Do my best," I finished. "I will." *So will Troy*, I thought with a sigh.

After breakfast Dad drove me out to the Double B to hitch up the trailer and get Gingersnap and our tack on board. As we drove the now-familiar dirt driveway to the stables, Troy saw us and waved. In his light denim jeans and jacket and black Stetson hat, he looked just like a real cowboy.

"Need any help with Gingersnap?" he asked, following me to the smaller barn. "I've already managed to coax Arrow into our trailer."

"Ginger's usually no trouble to load in the trailer." I held up crossed fingers. "Unless she's as nervous as I am."

Troy propped open the door to Gingersnap's stall while I slipped on her best halter and led her outside. "This is it, girl," I whispered in her ear. She whinnied her reply.

Troy laughed. "She seems a lot calmer than you do. Relax, Ronnie, this is supposed to be fun."

What happened to his nerves of yesterday? I wondered. *Is he so confident now that he'll win the blue that he doesn't have to worry?* I glanced at the relaxed smile on Troy's face, then turned back to my horse with renewed determination. With a light slap on her rump, Gingersnap went up the ramp into the trailer. Dad closed the tailgate and got back into the car.

"We'll follow you," he told Troy. "I'm not familiar with the towns around here yet."

It was still early, but we'd decided beforehand to let the horses get used to the Wellington grounds and to relax before the stress of competition. I was about to get into Dad's car when Troy motioned to me. "Hey, Ronnie, why don't you ride with me?" he called. "Mom is driving Dad out later so there's room here beside me."

I glanced at Dad, who shrugged. "Go ahead, Ronnie. I don't mind." He gave me a private wink. "See you there."

I guess that meant Dad approved of Troy. I leaned over to kiss his cheek, then ran to Troy's car. As we drove, I looked in the mirror outside my window every few minutes to be sure Dad was still behind us.

"You're going to wear out the rearview mirror," Troy said.

I leaned back against the seat. "I guess I'm being crazy, huh? It's just that I don't want anything to go wrong."

He looked over at me, his eyes smiling. "I know the feeling. You're not being crazy. My dad says if I'm not nervous about a show I won't do my best. So I guess these jitters are a good sign."

"But you don't seem jittery at all today," I remarked.

"Don't let this act fool you," Troy said. "Inside it feels like a convention of Mexican jumping beans."

I laughed. "I know what you mean. There must be quite a few jumping-bean conventions today."

"No kidding," Troy agreed, "you, me—and my dad." His face was serious now. All the tension of the day before seemed to have returned in full force.

I knew he felt that he had to win the blue for his father. I felt sorry for Troy. His father's car crash had changed his life too.

It was only a short ride to the sprawling Wellington Stables. My first glimpse of the neat white fences enclosing the many corrals made me gasp in awe.

"Troy, it's beautiful. This place looks like a postcard I have of a Kentucky horse farm. Look at that barn! It looks like a clubhouse or something." I pointed toward a long one-story building. It was neatly shingled and shuttered to match the enormous mansion nearby. Some people were already practicing in the various rings, while others were standing in groups talking. Cars and trailers filled a large field nearby. Every corral held several grazing horses. There was so much to see my head felt light. The air seemed to sizzle with excitement, especially when I saw the show ring decorated with festive banners and a bright yellow and green stand for the judges.

"This is fabulous!" I exclaimed.

Troy parked his car and we waited for Dad to pull into the spot beside us before getting out. I hurried over to open the trailer gate, but Gingersnap refused to back out.

"Come on, Ginger," I said softly. "Everything's okay. Just come on out now."

Ginger turned her head and looked at me with her big brown eyes, but still wouldn't budge. Suddenly Arrow whinnied behind us and Gingersnap's ears perked up. She moved backward with no problem.

I patted her silky smooth nose, laughing. "I know the feeling, girl. It's nice to have a friend close by."

Troy led Arrow closer to where we stood. "I'm going to walk him around for a few minutes to let him get used to the place. Do you and Ginger want to come?"

I nodded, then turned to Dad. He waved me off with a good-natured grin. "Go on. We want Ginger to be in top form this afternoon, don't we?" He reached out to pat Gingersnap on the neck. "Besides, your mother and grandmother will be here soon, so I'd better keep a lookout. If I don't see you again before the show . . . good lucky, honey." He kissed my cheek lightly.

Dad headed back to the entrance, while Troy, Arrow, Gingersnap, and I mingled with the others exercising their horses around the farm.

Even though there were still a few hours before show time, the place was teeming with people and horses. I had never seen so many different breeds in one place, nor so many colorful costumes. Excitement seemed to snap in the air like an electrical storm. I felt nervous, but happy to be a part of the excitement. Even when Troy and I became separated, I enjoyed wandering around on my own with Ginger by my side. Several times I caught a glimpse of him and Arrow across the field talking with other riders, and I felt a twinge of loneliness. Troy seemed to know so many people. Back in Indiana, I used to know lots of people at the shows, but here I knew only Troy. *Never mind, Ronnie,* I told myself. *This is only your first show. By the end of the summer, you'll know lots of people here too.*

Almost before I knew it, a voice over the loudspeaker announced that the show was about to begin. Although I already knew that I was scheduled to be the last rider in the Western Pleasure class, the last event of the day, I walked Gingersnap toward the show ring. I searched the grandstand for familiar faces, and immediately found Troy's parents looking grim in the front row. Behind them, Mom, Dad, and Gram were chattering excitedly, and nearby I was pleasantly surprised to see Lorie, Joe, Margaret, and Janet. I waved to them, and Lorie gave me a grin and a thumbs-up sign.

I stayed to watch the first few riders in the Eight and Under category, then I could feel Gingersnap getting restless.

"Okay, girl, calm down," I said as I led her away from the show ring. We headed for an empty corral not far away, and as we cantered around the field we left some of the tension of the competition behind us—for the moment, anyway.

I must have lost track of time, because the next thing I knew, the announcer was telling all entries for the Western Pleasure class to go to Gate B at the back of the show ring. Quickly I took hold of Ginger's reins and walked her to the designated gate. Troy was already there with Arrow. He didn't say anything, but gave me a pinched smile. I smiled back, those jumping beans going wild in my stomach again.

My self-confidence dangled by a thin thread as I watched rider after rider. All of them were good, especially Troy and Arrow. They demonstrated the different gaits for the judges without a hitch, and when Troy reined Arrow into a backward walk, Arrow seemed to respond instinctively.

After several more riders, it was my turn at last. The wait had increased my jitters considerably, and I could feel that Gingersnap was nervous too.

"Easy, girl," I crooned in her ear. "We can do it." The words were easy to say, but believing them was another story.

"I'd be crazy to say I hope you win," Troy said, giving me a lopsided grin as I rode past him. "But good luck, Ronnie."

I nodded just as my name was called. The late afternoon seemed suddenly warmer and I could feel beads of perspiration trickling down my forehead. When I rode into the ring, the people in the bleachers became a blur of moving colors. It was strange, a feeling I had never had before, even at the shows in Indiana. I automatically put Gingersnap through her walk, trot, and canter routine. As usual, she responded immediately to my touch. And when I reined her back, she stepped backward with very little guidance from me. I knew we had done well. Finally, Ginger walked the last stretch in front of the judges' stand. We left the ring to the sound of applause, lifting my morale up a few points.

"Not bad, Ronnie," Troy said quietly, riding alongside me. I blinked and looked around, the dazed feeling fading. "Come on," he urged. "We've all got to go back in the ring."

I nodded and turned Gingersnap around to follow the other entrants in the Western Pleasure class into the ring to line up in front of the judges' stand. My hands felt clammy holding the reins and my heart pounded as the judge's deep voice boomed out of the loud speaker.

"Fourth prize . . . Donna's Folly—ridden by Alice Magill . . ." We watched Alice smile her acknowledgment as the judge pinned a green ribbon to the Morgan mare's bridle.

Next the judge moved forward to pin a yellow ribbon on a jet-black gelding. His voice boomed, "Third prize . . . Rustler—ridden by Johnny Spruce."

My stomach tied in knots. I glanced at Troy. Anxiety was etched on his sun-bronzed face. Gingersnap and Arrow both stood silently as if they knew the moment of truth were at hand. The only motion in the lineup was the switching of the horses' tails.

"Second prize . . . Gingersnap—ridden by Veronica Wilson." I gulped as I watched him put the red ribbon on Gingersnap's bridle. I looked down at the ground in disappointment, but to my surprise, my disappointment didn't last long. Somehow second didn't seem so bad right now—especially for my first show in the area. There would be other shows and Gingersnap and I would continue to practice. Next time we would be ready to win the blue.

I could see the remaining riders waiting for the final outcome and I crossed my fingers. If I couldn't win the blue ribbon, then I wanted to see Troy get it. The judge moved slowly down the line of horses and riders as if he were enjoying the suspense, and finally stopped in front of Troy. Arrow stood still. Not even his tail moved as the announcer's voice boomed forth once again, this time to call out Troy's name.

Troy's friends applauded loudly. Glancing at the stands I noticed his parents cheering. Mr. Bennett had moved his wheelchair to the end of the bleachers and now raised his hat in the air, whistling his joy at Troy's win. I saw Troy smile in his father's direction and I guessed that all of Mr. Bennett's demanding coaching had paid off. Troy's win obviously meant a lot to him.

The stands emptied out quickly. A lot of people left the grounds, while others crowded around riders and their horses, snapping pictures and offering congratulations or condolences. Mom, Dad, Gram, and my friends joined me in the ring, and of course Mom pulled out her own trusty camera and started to click away. Their pride was evident. It didn't matter to them if I came in second, or fifth, or didn't win a thing. Everyone was congratulating me and telling me what a terrific ride I'd had.

I smiled happily as Dad offered Gingersnap a cube of sugar for a reward and patted her neck as she munched. She lifted her head high and whinnied at me. She seemed to be perfectly satisfied with her red ribbon.

Troy's parents and friends joined him and more cameras clicked. Excitement filled the air, and I let the pleasure of being at the show wash over me. I could feel my heart racing. My face felt warm, flushed from the thrill of competition.

"Come join me for a picture, Ronnie," Troy called.

Leaving Gingersnap with the others, I headed over to the fence where Troy was perched, talking to friends. "Nice going. I guess that's another blue for your collection, huh?" I teased.

He grinned at me, obviously pleased with himself. "It was close, Ronnie," he said, then a serious expression crossed his face. "No hard feelings?"

I shook my head. "Of course not."

"Good."

He glanced toward his mother who held a

small camera in her hands. "Snap one of us, will you, Mom?"

Mrs. Bennett obliged, then turned to talk to my parents and Gram. I noticed Mr. Bennett sitting off to the side clutching Arrow's reins in his hand. He had a faraway look in his eyes, and I guessed that he must have been thinking of the days when he won blue ribbons. I quickly looked away. I felt kind of selfish, but I refused to let Mr. Bennett's situation weaken my resolve to win a blue ribbon at the next show. By the end of summer *I'd* be hanging a blue ribbon in my room.

Chapter Nine

The loudspeaker whistled and Mr. Wellington's voice called, "Attention, riders. You all did a great job today, and it isn't over yet. We're having a barbecue and dance this evening, so feel free to turn your mounts out in the pasture and join in the fun."

When Troy looked my way, I wished I had the camera to capture him on film. He sat on the fence, face flushed, hat pushed back, sleeves rolled up, and his jeans dusty from his ride. When he smiled at me I felt myself melt. "How about it, Ronnie? Want to stay for the barbecue?"

"Sure," I exclaimed, my high spirits soaring even higher. "It sounds great."

"I'll take Gingersnap back to the farm," Dad told me. "We're going to be leaving for home now. If you need a ride give us a call." He kissed my cheek. "Nice riding today, honey."

"That goes for me too," Mom added.

"And me," Gram chimed in. "I'm glad I finally got to see you and Ginger in action. Next thing we know, you'll be in the Olympics."

I laughed. "Somehow I don't think so, Gram, but thanks anyway."

As I waved my parents and Gram goodbye, Lorie nudged my arm.

"Lorie, I'm sorry. I haven't had much chance to talk to you guys today."

She gave me a mischievous grin. "That's okay. We understand."

"Will you at least stay for the barbecue?" I asked.

"I don't think so," she said in a low voice. "Tonight might be your big chance with Troy, and we don't want to get in the way."

Before I could protest, Lorie and the others had said their goodbyes, and I was left alone with Troy.

"Shall we get in line for some dinner?" Troy suggested.

I nodded and followed him to the large patio behind the mansion, where chicken pieces were sizzling on a giant grill and a long table was covered with platters of salads, chili, and rolls. We filled up our plates and brought them to a quiet corner of the yard.

"I don't believe all this food," I remarked.

"The Wellingtons do this every year," Troy said. "It's sort of a tradition—the first show of the summer."

After that, we didn't talk much as we dug

into the delicious food. I couldn't help giving Troy surreptitious glances every now and then as I thought about Lorie's parting words. Would tonight turn out to be my big chance? After tonight, would I be Troy's girlfriend and not just a plain old friend?

Troy finished his chicken and glanced up to find me looking at him. I blushed, but he didn't seem to notice.

"How about some dessert?" he asked, taking my hand to pull me up. We walked back over to the patio, hand in hand, just as we had that day we had the picnic underneath the willow tree, and my hand felt warm and comfortable in his. As we weaved our way through the crowd, our eyes met for a brief moment, and Troy squeezed my hand gently. My heart soared. Had he been thinking the same thing I had?

When we reached the dessert table, I saw a huge chocolate cake in the shape of a horse. I'd never seen anything like it.

"They've really outdone themselves this year," Troy remarked.

I nodded, and knew my eyes were as big as saucers as Mr. Wellington cut the cake. Chocolate is on the top of my list of favorite foods, and this cake looked extra gooey and delicious. It was a good thing that Troy held my hand as we returned to our corner of the yard with the dessert plates, or I probably would have finished my piece before we even got there.

As we were savoring the last of our cake, I noticed two girls heading our way. I recognized them as two of the people I had seen Troy talking to before the show. Although I hadn't thought twice about it then, the girls were making me nervous now.

"Hi, Troy," said the tall brunette, pulling her blond friend up next to her.

"Hi, Angie," Tony replied with a friendly smile. "Hi, Barb. Do you two know Ronnie Wilson?"

"Nice to meet you," I said, putting on a false smile.

The girls nodded at me politely, then ignored me.

"Go on, Barb," the tall brunette whispered, giving her friend a nudge.

Barb hesitated. "Um, Troy, Angie and I and a few others are taking off to the movies now, and, uh, I was wondering if you wanted to go."

I couldn't believe the nerve of those girls, but Troy didn't seem bothered. *I don't get it*, I thought, bristling with anger. *Was he only spending time with me until something better came along?*

"How about it?" he asked, looking at me. "Do you want to go to the movies, Ronnie?"

"Troy, I think Barb just meant you," Angie cut in quickly.

I was really angry now. Couldn't they see that he was with me? And why didn't he *say* something? "Troy, if you want to go to the movies, go ahead," I finally said in an off-hand tone. "I don't mind."

He gave me a puzzled look. "But how will you get home?"

"I'm sure someone at home will come pick me up," I snapped, turning away. I couldn't believe it. His only reason for turning down their invitation was because he felt obligated to take me home. Just great.

"Will you come with us then?" Barb asked, her eyes lighting up in anticipation.

Troy looked down at the crumbs on his plate. "No, I don't think so. But thanks anyway."

I gave a deep sigh of relief.

"Oh, come on, Troy," Angie coaxed. "Your friend says she doesn't mind."

"I know, but I still think I'd rather stay here," he said.

The look of disappointment on Barb's face was priceless. I might have even felt sorry for her if it had been some other boy she'd been asking to the movies.

After the girls left, Troy and I were both quiet. Music was playing on the patio now and it looked like several people were dancing.

"Did you really not mind if I went to the movies with Barb and Angie?" Troy asked at last, sounding hurt.

I shrugged uncomfortably. "Those girls sounded like they were going to have a good time. I didn't want you to feel you *had* to stay on account of me."

"Barb and Angie aren't my type. Besides," he added with a smile, "I *want* to stay here on account of you."

I looked up, meeting his brown eyes. "Me too," I said. "I mean, I want to stay here with you."

Troy leaned over and kissed me lightly on the lips. "I'm glad we agree." He put out his hand. "And now Miss Wilson, may I have this dance?"

"I have two left feet," I reminded him, as I got up from my seat on the ground.

"That's okay, I have two right feet." He turned to me laughing. "But haven't we been through this before?" I nodded. "Well, if you don't care, I don't care. We'll just have to warn people not to get in our way."

"It's a deal," I said.

We had a wonderful time dancing. Troy wasn't as bad a dancer as he'd made out, and I wasn't as bad as I'd always thought either. The disc jockey played all sorts of music, from rock to rap, and even a little country Western, but my favorites were the slow romantic songs when Troy would put his arms around me and hold me close.

If Lorie could see us now, I thought, smiling contentedly. *She was right all along. And so what if I didn't get the blue ribbon today. I got the best consolation prize in the whole world!*

Chapter Ten

The following morning I phoned Lorie as soon as I had showered and dressed. A very groggy voice came over the line.

"Hello?" Lorie mumbled sleepily.

"Lorie, it's me—Ronnie," I said impatiently. I was dying to tell her about last night.

But instead of a battery of questions, all I heard was a long pause.

"Lorie, are you there? Come on, wake up," I urged. "Don't you want to know what happened after you left Wellington Farm last night?"

"Wellington Farm?" she echoed, as if she were digesting the information. Suddenly her voice came through loud and clear. "Ronnie, something happened with Troy, didn't it?" she shrieked.

I laughed. Now that was the sort of reaction I'd expected.

"Why don't you come horseback riding with me today and I'll tell you about it," I suggested. "It's Sunday, so you can put your job search on hold."

"But I haven't been riding since I took those lessons a million years ago," Lorie protested.

"Don't worry, they've got a few beginners' horses at the Double B, and we'll go on an easy trail," I told her. "You *do* want to know what happened with Troy, don't you?" I added in my most mysterious voice.

"That's blackmail, Wilson," Lorie said, giggling. "But I'll be there."

When we arrived at the farm, I was disappointed to find that Troy wasn't around. Mr. Bennett had the stable hand saddle up Old Ben for Lorie and we took off on a trail through the woods. Old Ben had one favorite speed—a slow plod—so I kept Gingersnap closely reined in. The slow pace gave Lorie and me a good chance to talk. She was thrilled about my progress with Troy.

"Slow dances are so romantic, aren't they?" she remarked as we turned the horses around to head back to the stables.

"Definitely," I replied with a smile. I was still smiling and recalling the feel of Troy's arms around me, when I felt Ginger take an awkward step and stumble. As we rode on I noticed she was limping so I dismounted and checked her left front hoof which she seemed to favor. I walked her slowly and watched that leg. The limp was less noticeable, but still there, and her knee seemed a bit swollen as well.

"Darn!" I exclaimed. "Looks like I"m going to have to lead her back to the barn. You can ride on ahead if you want to."

Lorie shook her head. "Are you kidding? Even lame Gingersnap can beat Speedy Gonzales here." She patted Old Ben's brown neck. "Will Gingersnap be all right?"

"I hope so," I said quietly. "I'll soak her leg and let her rest today and see what happens. If it isn't okay tomorrow I'll call the vet." I was hopeful there would be no problem. Poor Gingersnap—I hated to see her in pain. Also, I'd been planning to enter the show at Washburn Stables on the following Saturday. If only I'd been paying more attention to the trails, instead of thinking about Troy . . . I shook my head. No use worrying about that now.

When Lorie and I returned to the stables Mr. Bennett was saddle-soaping a bridle on a table inside the barn. He looked up as I lead Gingersnap inside.

"What happened?" he asked, noticing the mare's limp.

"She stepped in a hole," I told him. "Her knee seems a little swollen."

He wheeled his chair closer, reaching down to run his hand over Gingersnap's leg. "Just a little pull," he said. "She'll be fine, but if I were you I'd give her a rest for a couple of days to be on the safe side."

I nodded. "Thanks for checking her for me. I don't know what I'd do if anything happened to Gingersnap."

Tires squealed in the barnyard and through the stable window I could see Troy leap out of his car. Mr. Bennett patted the mare on her side and swung his wheelchair around to go outside. "I'm glad you're home, son. Mike had to leave early today so the work has piled up." He chuckled at the pun. "Can you manage it? I know you want to work with Arrow so you can make a good showing Saturday."

I saw a flash of disappointment in Troy's dark eyes. "It's no problem, Dad. If I'd known Mike had to leave early today, I would have skipped this morning's swim with the guys."

"No need for that, you're here now," Mr. Bennett said. He nodded toward the large barn where Lorie and I were. "Unsaddle Old Ben first. Then I guess you can clean the stalls. If there's time later I'll watch you work Arrow backing up through the poles. I had Mike set them up for you in the ring before he left," Mr. Bennett said.

Troy nodded, brushing past him into the barn to unsaddle Old Ben while I removed the saddle, blanket, and pad from Gingersnap's back. "Hi, you two," he greeted us, then immediately noticed the way Gingersnap stood favoring her leg. "What's wrong with her?"

"She stepped in a hole while we were out riding," I told him. "Thank goodness it wasn't a chuckhole or her leg could be a lot worse."

He bent down to gently feel Gingersnap's leg as his father had done. "Maybe we can get her in shape by Saturday, Ronnie. If not, there will be other shows."

Easy for him to say, I thought.

He saw my crestfallen look, "Hey, I didn't mean to sound like a jerk. I know you want to be in that show. Tell you what. I'll spend extra time with compresses and give Gingersnap Dr. Bennett's special TLC." He gave me one of his super smiles. "At no extra cost, of course."

"That would be great!" I looked at Lorie, who stood quietly rubbing Old Ben's white blaze. "What do you say we lend Troy a helping hand?"

Her eyes widened in mock horror. "Mucking out stalls? Me?"

"Sure, why not? Troy, if you take care of Gingersnap we'll do some shoveling. Fair?" I pulled a sugar cube from my pocket and fed it to my mare, then gave one to Old Ben.

Troy nodded. "Sounds like a fair deal to me." He nodded toward the pitchforks and shovels hanging on the wall. "Have fun."

Mr. Bennett wheeled over to us. "Nice try,"

he told his son, "but it won't work. I can handle the mare's compresses. I think one of those pitchforks has your name on it." A smile crinkled the corners of his eyes as he spoke.

Troy moaned. "See what I have to put up with?"

Lorie and I grabbed shovels, laughing as we shouldered them. "Poor Troy," I said. "Bet we can shovel faster than you."

I didn't see much of Troy for the next few days. I stopped by the stables every morning, but only for an hour or so to make sure Gingersnap was okay. Although she seemed in good spirits, she was still limping slightly and I knew we'd have to miss the Washburn show.

Arrow, on the other hand, was training well. Troy had decided to enter the Trail Horse class at Washburn, which meant that he had to teach Arrow to go through and around various obstacles. And when Troy wasn't practicing in the ring, he was busy doing chores around the farm. He didn't seem to have much time for me at all. He was always friendly when we did run into each other at the stables, but that was as far as it went. Once I even offered to help with his chores, but Troy said he'd rather do it himself. My hopes of romance that had soared after the Wellington barbecue now plummeted.

I simply couldn't understand Troy's attitudes, and by Friday I was fed up. So when Lorie suggested we go job hunting in town, I agreed. I was sure I could work a part-time job and still have enough time to spend with Gingersnap. Besides, I was still feeling guilty about the bills for Ginger's board at the Double B, and if I had a job I'd be able to help. I'd also be keeping busy—and keeping my mind off Troy.

I put my case to my parents at breakfast that morning.

"We appreciate your offering, but it's not really necessary," Mom said.

"I agree with your mother, Veronica." Dad always called me by my full name when he was being serious. "I think you should take this summer to enjoy riding. Between your mother's salary and mine we can take care of Ginger's board."

"But I want to get a job," I said.

My parents exchanged a glance. "It's up to you, Ronnie," Mom said. "But don't rush into it. Why don't you just go along with Lorie today, then decide."

"Okay," I agreed. "Maybe that's a good idea."

Actually, I was already going off the idea of a job. Staying indoors behind a desk or a shop counter when the sun was shining outside didn't really appeal to me. I'd much rather spend my summer with Gingersnap. I'd go into town with Lorie today since I'd already promised, but I'd bring a book to read while I was waiting.

Lorie arrived at ten o'clock right on schedule. When I told her I'd just be a passenger today, her blue eyes widened in surprise.

"Lucky you! My dad practically pushed me out the door. He wished me luck, but I think he really wanted to say, 'Don't come back unless you have a job.' "

I laughed. "I doubt that." I'd met Lorie's dad. He seemed like a laid-back type of person who never seemed to let things bother him—a lot like my dad.

We parked in the town lot and Lorie started off on her quest. I pulled a paperback out of my shoulder bag and settled down under a shady maple tree on the edge of the lot. I didn't pay much attention to the people coming and going as I flipped the pages, eager to find out what would happen to Pegasus, the heroic racehorse in my book. I guess I'd been reading for about an hour when I heard a familiar voice call to me from the sidewalk.

"Hey, Ronnie, what are you doing here?"

I turned to look toward the road and spotted Troy sitting in the Bennett's pickup truck. He didn't wait for me to reply, but got out, inserted some coins in the parking meter and bounded over the low hedge to join me. My first reaction was genuine pleasure in seeing him, but I quickly remembered his recent attitude toward me and decided I'd better be on my guard.

"Hi, Troy," I said. I held my book in front of me as if I was reluctant to put it down, but he didn't seem to notice.

"I haven't seen much of you lately," Troy remarked.

I shrugged. "I guess we've both been busy."

"Yeah." He nodded thoughtfully. "Are you going to come to the Washburn show? Arrow and I are entered in the Trail Horse class."

"I know," I said. "I saw you practicing in the ring on Tuesday, remember?"

Troy's face looked blank.

"I guess you were too busy to notice."

Troy looked away in what I hoped was embarrassment.

"You know, I've been hoping all week that Gingersnap would be ready to ride so you could be in the show." He pulled up a long piece of grass and chewed on the end. "You could have worked with one of our horses, you know."

"I know," I said. "I promised Ginger a long time ago she was the only horse I'd ride. I can't go back on that promise."

"No, I guess not." He grinned. "A lot of people would say you're crazy, you know."

"Only those who don't love horses." I looked

up and caught his eye. "Do you know this is the first time we've had a proper conversation all week?"

His brown eyes softened. "Have I been that much of a jerk lately? Look, I'm sorry, Ronnie. I've been in a fog, I guess. I know he means well, but sometimes I feel like Dad is cracking a whip over my back. I don't have much time to think of anything except training with Arrow and mucking out stables. With him it's win, win, work, win. That's what keeps him going." He took a deep breath and stared at the ground for a moment. "Hey, you didn't answer my original question. What are you doing sitting under a tree in the town parking lot?"

"Lorie is job hunting, so I came along for the ride. She should be back here soon." I held up my crossed fingers. "Here's hoping. I know she really wants a job, and she's been getting a lot of pressure at home. I, on the other hand, have been told I should enjoy this summer with Gingersnap."

Troy tossed down the piece of grass. "Your folks are great, Ronnie. You're lucky."

Lorie returned as we spoke, looking dejected. "Nothing," she exclaimed. "The lady in the dress shop suggested I go up the street to the antique shop." She wrinkled her nose. "I did. But, I don't think I'd like to work around moldy old furniture. It wouldn't be much fun."

"So what's your plan now?"

"I'm going to drive over to Henrietta. I should be able to find a job in one of the stores in the mall. Want to come along?" When I didn't answer right away, Lorie glanced at Troy and gave me a secret smile. "You don't have to if you don't want. You'll probably have a better time at the Double B."

"Hey, that's a good idea," Troy agreed. "I have some errands to do in town, but if you don't mind waiting, I'll take you back to the Double B in a few minutes. Dad said you can ride Gingersnap in the ring today if you take it easy. I'd guess she'd even be ready to enter the show at the Bronson Stables next week. How about it? You don't mind riding in the truck, do you?"

"Of course not." I wanted to tell him I'd ride in a covered wagon if he was along. I turned to Lorie. "Call me later, okay? And, good luck."

She nodded, heading for her car. "Will do. 'Bye, you two. Have fun mucking out those stalls."

Lorie knew that any time I spent with Troy was fun, even cleaning stalls. "That's not such a bad idea," I told him. "I'll be glad to lend a hand. The work will get done quicker with two of us."

Troy grinned at me. "I'll accept your help. That way I can put in more time in the saddle. There are a lot more blue ribbons out there waiting for me."

He was kidding, but his words made me wince. "You already have enough to cover a wall," I reminded him. Suddenly I was more determined than ever to win. "Now it's *my* turn."

Why do we always end up talking about blue ribbons? I wondered. *Doesn't he realize that I offered to help him out so we could spend more time together? I wasn't even thinking about blue ribbons.* I gave a determined sigh. *But if that's the way he wants it, then he'd better watch out, because it's Veronica Wilson who's going to win the blue ribbon at the Bronson show—not Troy Bennett.*

Chapter Eleven

With that thought in mind, the rest of the day passed quickly. When we got to the stables Troy and I grabbed shovels, pitchforks, and wheelbarrows and went to work. Troy started at one end of the barn, and I started at the other. By the time we met in the middle the stalls were clean with fresh straw. We stood back to admire our work.

"One thing is certain," Troy said, laughing as he pulled a piece of straw from my hair. "We'll never have to worry about being out of a job. We're both pretty good with these pitchforks."

"My claim to fame," I told him, rubbing my nose to stop an itch. It was too late. The sneeze echoed through the barn. One of the horses down the hall gave a shrill whinny. "Sorry about that," I sniffed. "Straw dust does that to me sometimes."

"At least you're not allergic to Gingersnap."

"Bite your tongue, Troy Bennett," I warned him. "That would be a king-size disaster."

He picked up another piece of straw from my hair. "You'd just have to learn to ride as you sneeze," he joked, then looked at me a moment. "Are you tired yet?"

"If that's a nice way of asking if I'm up to more work, the answer is yes. I can work as long and hard as you." I put my hands on my hips. "So what's the next job?"

He took two brushes from a shelf in the tack room. "The horses could stand a little TLC."

He tossed one of the brushes at me, but as I reached out to catch it I felt another sneeze coming on.

"Ah-ah-ah-choo!" The force of the sneeze jerked my body forward and miraculously the brush fell into my hand.

Troy gazed at me in awe. "Wow, that was really good. Can you do that again?"

I giggled. "I doubt it," I said, turning to the horses and the work at hand.

I always enjoyed grooming horses, watching their dusty coats turn sleek under my hand. We worked at the corral fence, combing and brushing until our arms ached. I talked softly to the horses, while Troy whistled an off-key tune. Finally, I led Gingersnap over to the fence to brush her and comb her mane and tail. I could tell from the way she whinnied softly and pawed the ground that she was eager to go out for a ride. I stroked her neck and talked to her, assuring her she would be running again soon.

When I finished with Gingersnap Troy motioned to me from the corral. "I'm going to saddle Arrow and get busy again."

I watched him practice figure eights and backups until Mr. Bennett came out to take up his coaching position in the viewing room. Then I felt in the way and decided it was time to go home. I had to admit Troy and Arrow made a terrific team even if they couldn't do perfect figure eights. I was almost glad I wouldn't be competing this time.

I called home from the phone in the tack room. I didn't want to bother Troy. I knew if I asked he would stop riding and take me home, and I didn't think his father would appreciate that.

Mom had just gotten home from work. "I still have the car keys in my hand," she said. "I'll be right there."

I left while Troy was still backing Arrow in and out between lined up poles. He was so intent on what he was doing that I didn't think he'd realize I had gone. It was clear by now that if I wanted to stick with Troy, I'd always be second place to winning those blue ribbons.

*   *   *

After supper I phoned Lorie. She answered in her usual perky voice. "Hello . . . Lorie here. Who's there?"

"I'm here," I laughed. "How was job hunting?"

"Well I have two interviews next week. And I had one this afternoon at a shoe store. They wanted to hire me, but, Ronnie . . ." She moaned. "When I thought of putting shoes on people's feet all day I said no thanks. I'll wait and hope for something in the bookstore, or better still, maybe the record store."

"You'd be perfect working in a record store," I told her. "You know a lot about music."

"I hope the manager agrees," Lorie said, then she paused for a long moment. "I want to do something, have some fun. Why don't we go to a movie tomorrow night? There are two new ones starting in Henrietta. I suppose Joe will want to see *The Monster from Mars*, but maybe I can convince him to see Charlie King in that *Wild Dance* movie."

I wrinkled my nose. "Neither one sounds great to me. You're the rock fan, not me. You and Joe go ahead. I'd just be a third wheel."

She sounded surprised. "What about Troy?"

"Who knows. Right now he's more interested in winning at the Washburn show. If he does get a blue ribbon I'm sure he'd go, if not . . ." I shrugged. "I wouldn't bet on it."

"Aren't you going to go to the show?" Lorie askd.

"Why should I?" I replied ruefully. "I can't enter Gingersnap, and Troy probably wouldn't know the difference if I was there or not. He's too concerned with his ribbons."

"You have a problem," Lorie declared.

I sighed. "Tell me about it."

It was late on Saturday when Troy phoned. I had just finished washing my hair and it was dripping wet. I wrapped a towel around my head before I answered the phone. "I had to call," he said without even a hello. "I hope you don't mind. I know it's late."

I could tell by the sound of his voice that something was wrong, so I put aside my irritation. "How did you do today?" I asked him.

He moaned. "You shouldn't ask. It was a disaster, Ronnie. We got a green. I was sure we'd at least get a red. It's a good thing you weren't there. You know how hard I worked with Arrow on those figure eights. Well, he tripped over his own feet. No kidding, Ronnie. He was a first class klutz today. Dad told me I should have entered the kids' class." Troy sighed, sounding tired.

I couldn't help feeling sorry for Troy. He tried so hard. Maybe too hard. He should know that no one can win all the time. "I'm sure you'll do fine next week. I'll be there, remember. Maybe you just missed my cheery face today." I laughed, hoping to raise his morale.

"As a matter of fact," he said quietly, "I did miss you."

His words made me feel good. *Maybe I should have gone to the show,* I thought. "We'll both be riding at the Bronson Stables next week. That's something to look forward to," I said. "What class are you entering? I know my limitations so I'll stick to Western Pleasure."

"After today's disaster I think that's my best bet too," he said, sounding more cheerful. "So, I guess we'll be competing again."

I took a deep breath. "I guess so." I laughed. "We're tough. We can handle it, right?"

"Ronnie, let's make the same deal we made before the Wellington show," Troy suggested. "No hard feelings, no matter who wins, okay?"

"It's a deal," I replied, smiling into the telephone receiver. But I couldn't help wondering if he'd feel the same if I won the blue.

Troy and I practiced in the ring every afternoon that week. Usually his father sat in his wheelchair watching, handing out more advice and criticism to Troy. By now I was used to his method of coaching Troy, and simply did my best to ignore his comments. I was just glad that he didn't direct any of his comments to me.

I could tell that the rest had done Gingersnap good. She responded well to every touch of my knees and every flick of the reins. By the end of the week I was sure she was ready to win us a blue ribbon. I had never felt it so strongly before, and instead of feeling apprehensive, I couldn't wait for the show. While we both practiced hard, I still tried to keep things light. But Troy rode with his usual desperate drive, and the fun we'd had when we first began to ride together had vanished. Now, it was as if a cloud had dropped between us. Was Troy afraid I would win? Would my taking a blue ribbon change our relationship? I didn't like to think so, but things had definitely changed—little things, like a look, a smile, a touch . . . and I missed them. I wondered if Troy remembered our deal. After all, it had been his idea. But I could only assume from his behavior that either he had forgotten, or he simply didn't care anymore.

The day of the Bronson show was cloudy and muggy without a breeze stirring. The humidity was high, the kind Gram said you could cut with a knife. But not even the weather could upset my mood. For a change,

I felt confident that this was going to be a good day.

Later at the Double B when Dad and I arrived to get Gingersnap, she must have felt the same way. She was up into the trailer so quickly that Dad laughed. "If that mare was human I'd say she was in a hurry to get to the horse show."

I closed the trailer gate. "She's good and she knows it," I said. "And today she's going to prove it."

A crowd had already gathered by the time Dad pulled the trailer into the driveway at the Bronson Stables. I glanced around hoping to see Troy. I knew he and his father had left the Double B early so Troy could warm up before the show. For some reason winning this show seemed to mean even more to him than the others. When we met at the fence later I decided to find out why.

"Well, here we go again." I tried to sound cheerful. "May the best man—or woman— win."

He hunched his shoulders. "Yeah."

I scowled. "Okay, Troy Bennett, start talking. I know you've been nervous before the other shows, but this one has you really uptight. I want to know why."

"Just because," he said with a shrug.

"Well, that's a good answer," I replied sarcastically. "Listen, Troy, all week I've put up with your frowns and your moody silences, and frankly I'm sick of it." I stopped abruptly, surprised at my outburst. I hadn't meant to say all that.

Troy sighed, pounding his fist on the fence. "Sorry, I didn't realize I was taking it out on you. You see, Dad was on his way to ride in the Bronson show the day of his accident. He'd come in first in every one he entered that year, and this was the last one of the season. I think it still bothers him that he didn't get the chance to compete. It's like unfinished business. So you see, I really want this one."

So that was the problem. Guilt bubbled inside me. Was I being selfish? I wanted to win too. For a minute my feelings were jumbled. Finally, I shook my head. It was a competition, wasn't it? Everyone who entered wanted to win. If Gingersnap and I gave the best performance, we had every right to the blue ribbon.

Troy and I stayed at the fence to watch the events in round one. We mounted up just before the Open Western Pleasure class. Again I was the last rider in the class, but this time I didn't mind waiting. I was glad I'd be able to see how the other entrants rode before my turn. The first three were okay, but I knew I could do better. Then Troy's name was called. I gave him a quick smile, then watched anxiously as he entered the ring. He rode well, guiding Arrow smoothly through his gaits. He looked like a winner until the canter, when Arrow hesitated a second and tossed his head. I couldn't believe it—I'd never seen Arrow stumble like that in practice. Troy's face showed his frustration and disappointment. I bit my lip, wondering how the stumble would affect the judges' evaluation.

I didn't have long to think about it. My name was called and I gave Gingersnap an encouraging pat on the neck when we entered the ring. She responded quickly to every touch of my knees and flick of the reins. Each change in gait was smooth and even. I felt as if Ginger were a part of me, that the four legs moving in rhythm around the ring were mine. I knew we were good and it was a terrific feeling. The blue ribbon was mine.

I glanced up and saw Troy watching, looking kind of dejected. When he saw me glance at him he gave me the a-okay sign, but without his usual smile of encouragement. All of a sudden, my feelings were all jumbled up. I thought about what Troy had said earlier about wanting this win for his father.

Gingersnap kept up her gaits perfectly—I didn't even have to do anything, which was good because my heart wasn't in it anymore. Troy would have taken the blue ribbon if Arrow hadn't stumbled. I caught a brief glimpse of Mr. Bennett watching me as I rode past. Like Troy, his expression was sad. Were they both remembering another horse show at this very stable years ago? A show Mr. Bennett was unable to enter?

Suddenly I knew what I had to do. Just before I was to urge Gingersnap into a full gallop, I touched her leg lightly three times. Immediately she slowed her gait and went into her limping act. I stopped her and dismounted, shaking my head at the judge. The speaker boomed forth my name and number, announcing regrets that Gingersnap and I were unable to continue in the competition. From the corner of my eye I saw Mr. Bennett whirl around in his chair. He pushed his way to the fence as I led Gingersnap out of the ring, but Troy stood back from the fence, holding Arrow's reins. I thought Troy would be happy. After all, he was just about certain to win the blue ribbon now. But his face was set in a fierce scowl as I led Gingersnap past him. Once out of the ring Gingersnap dropped her lame act and I let her graze in the lush grass near the first paddock.

Troy swung up into the saddle, urging Arrow into a trot. He reined in next to me.

"What was that all about?" I could see the anger in his dark eyes.

I shrugged. "Gingersnap's leg bothered her again. I guess I rode her too soon," I told him.

He snorted. "Don't give me that, Ronnie. She was favoring the wrong leg just now."

The speaker blared, "Western Pleasure class riders line up in the ring."

Troy glared at me, pulled Arrow around and headed for the ring. I turned away, walking Ginger near the paddock so I couldn't see the riders in the ring. I was glad I'd forfeited the ribbon, but that didn't stop the hurt. A few minutes later Troy rode up with the shiny blue ribbon attached to Arrow's bridle. My stomach felt achy. That ribbon looked so beautiful. I managed a smile. "Congratulations," I said. "I knew you'd win."

He jumped to the ground in front of me. "Thanks to you." His tone was angry. "Look, Ronnie, I know you made Gingersnap go into her lame act. Maybe no one else knew it was a phony limp, but I sure did."

I shrugged, trying to act casual. "I know how much your winning meant to your father. Besides, Gingersnap and I might not have won anyway."

He ran his hand over Arrow's neck, glaring at me. "You were number one and you know it. You did a dumb thing, throwing the show

122

like that. Now Dad thinks I won. I feel as if I'm lying to him, thanks to you, and I hate it." He whirled around, leading Arrow back toward his parents. "Thanks for *nothing!*" he yelled over his shoulder.

My stomach churned. I had never seen Troy so angry. Tears stung my eyes. It wasn't the reaction I thought he would have. He was right. It was a dumb thing for me to do, but I couldn't undo it now. And I had done it for him. I blinked back the tears. I had the terrible feeling Troy would never speak to me again.

Thankfully, no one else seemed to know what I had done. Mom, Dad, and Gram were all sorry I had lost and they hoped Gingersnap was okay. I was feeling more guilty and depressed by the minute. I was glad when we got the mare into the trailer, ready to drive her back to the Double B. Glad until Dad shut the gate, that is.

"She's fine now," he said quietly. "No sign of a limp." He turned to look at me and I swallowed hard.

"You know." I sighed.

He nodded. "I knew the minute she went lame. I watched you train her, remember? Why did you do it, Ronnie? You'd definitely have gotten the blue."

I tried to explain about Mr. Bennett's accident, and Troy wanting to win for his father.

And I told him about how my plan had only made Troy hate me.

"Not really," Dad said. "He'll realize why you did it. Give him time. It *was* wrong, you know. But, for what it's worth, I'm proud of you." He leaned down and kissed my forehead. "Now, let's get home."

I went to join Mom and Gram in the car, my stomach still tight with fear. Would Troy realize what I'd done for him? Dad said he'd forgive me, but right now I didn't believe he would.

Chapter Twelve

I was right. In the days following the horse show, the atmosphere at the Double B was like winter in Iceland. Troy avoided me when he could, and when our paths did cross, he'd give me a "hi" that was as cool as a snowball. If I tried to say more he'd walk away, not hearing a word I said. Finally I gave up. Dad, Mom, or Gram drove me to the Double B every day and picked me up. I rode Ginger-snap, groomed her, and didn't stay at the stables longer than necessary. I hated it. All the fun of earlier weeks was gone.

Troy seemed to be busier than ever, giving riding lessons, taking groups on trail rides, and hanging out with his friends, as well as doing his regular chores at the stables. I suspected he was trying to avoid me. And although the next horse show wasn't scheduled for several more weeks, Troy seemed to be training with a vengeance. I felt lost and lonely. If only he'd give me a chance to explain, I was sure we could work things out.

On top of all this, Lorie had gotten the job at the record store and worked nearly every day, so I didn't see much of her. We talked on the phone every night but we didn't get together much. She was always tired from working, or was out with Joe. I did see her one night after supper and told her about the disaster that had taken place. She listened, but what could she say?

"You shouldn't have done it," she told me.

I knew that now. Days began to drag and I began to feel very sorry for myself. The fun had gone out of the summer.

A few nights later Lorie phoned with a great idea. "Let's spend Saturday afternoon at the mall in Henrietta," she suggested.

I practically jumped for joy. "It sounds perfect," I told her. My spirits rose a bit at the thought of spending some time with a friend. It had been the worst week of my life. I wished Gingersnap was back in Gram's yard. Then I wouldn't have to go out to the Double B to see her.

"No gloom from now on, Ronnie," Lorie said as soon as I got into the car. "Let's enjoy ourselves."

And enjoy ourselves we did. For the whole afternoon I managed to distance myself from thoughts of Troy and the dumb thing I had done. First we went to Sibley's, one of the largest department stores in the area, where

Lorie bought a new blouse to go with her denim miniskirt.

"I'm spending my first paycheck on me," she declared. "Joe and I are going to a concert at the auditorium in Rochester next Saturday night and I want to look great."

I nodded. "You always look great." Lorie's hobby was clothes. Mine was Gingersnap.

"Take my advice," she said. "If you're feeling down, buy something new."

I laughed. "For my soul?"

She gave me a quizzical look. "What?"

"That's what Gram says when she buys something she doesn't need. She says it's for her soul. Something to make her feel good."

"So, do it," Lorie urged, clutching her Sibley's bag and poking through the rack of blouses. "Here's one that's you," she said, pointing to a blue denim cotton shirt with a paisley design on the collar.

I took it from the rack and held it out. "Not bad. I could wear it riding. . . ." It was on sale, marked down twenty-five percent. Before I knew it, I, too, clutched a Sibley's bag. I didn't really need the blouse, but Lorie was right. Buying it had boosted my sagging morale. For a little while at least I didn't think about Troy and how much I missed him.

The days dragged on. Sometimes I wished I had gone through with my idea and found a job just as Lorie had. At least then I would have had something to do besides going to the Double B. I still loved to go there to see Gingersnap, but whenever I saw Troy at the stables my hands went clammy and my stomach churned. I couldn't stand not talking to him. The few times I tried he turned away. I might as well have been invisible for all the attention he gave me. I even thought about finding another place to board Gingersnap. It would be easier not to have to see Troy every day and pretend we were strangers.

One sunny afternoon I decided to take Gingersnap jumping. I had started to take her over low jumps back in Indiana, so I knew she could do it. Perhaps if we practiced enough, we'd be able to compete in the jumping class at some shows next year. I wanted to enter as many shows as I could next summer, and go into different classes, so I decided it was time to find out just what Gingersnap could do. I also hoped it would help my low morale to teach her new things. She seemed to sense that I was eager to try her in a new activity and stamped her hooves impatiently, eager to tackle the jumps.

I was relieved to notice that Troy wasn't around. He would only have made me nervous. I knew that the three cars in the yard belonged to his friends, and I had also noticed several horses missing from the stable. Troy had probably organized another trail ride, so he wouldn't be back for some time.

Gingersnap and I had been jumping for several hours when Mr. Bennett rolled his chair over to the fence to watch me. Seeing him there made my hands go clammy, and since I could no longer concentrate on my riding, I decided to quit for the day.

I was surprised when Mr. Bennett met me at the gate. "Not bad," he said, smiling up at me. Before I could thank him for the compliment his smile vanished and concern etched his face. "Is something going on between you and Troy? He's been in a mighty dark mood since that show a couple of weeks ago. Whenever your name is mentioned he clams up. And it doesn't take a genius to see that the two of you never ride together these days."

I shrugged, avoiding his gaze. "We had a disagreement," I told him. I certainly didn't intend to tell Mr. Bennett that our disagreement had come about because of him.

He nodded. "That happens. I hope you can work it out."

He headed toward the small barn to talk to a boarder who was busy grooming her palomino, while I went into the tack room to phone home. Gram answered on the second ring.

"I hate to ask," I began, "but is the family

taxi available? Don't worry, soon I'll have my driver's license and I won't bother anyone for a ride."

"Nonsense," Gram said good-naturedly into the phone. "It's no bother. Besides, it gives me a chance to talk with my favorite grand-daughter. I'll be there in a few minutes."

I laughed. "I'm your *only* granddaughter. I'll be waiting."

Grooming Gingersnap passed the time until Gram arrived. I felt good about my practice session. The wheels in my head began to spin. Maybe in the fall I might try jumping her in a proper English dressage—nothing too difficult, but it would be fun to work on something totally new. Troy could go on with his barrel races and pole bending. At least we wouldn't be competing against each other if we entered different events. And if I found another home for Gingersnap, we wouldn't get in each other's way in the practice ring.

I saw Troy and his friends return from their trail ride as Gram drove into the yard. Quickly I turned Gingersnap out into the pasture with the other horses and scrambled into Gram's car just as the riding group came into the backyard. I saw Troy glance our way, and at the sight of him my heart felt like lead in my chest. I wanted to wave, but I was afraid he would ignore me, so I didn't do anything. He looked so handsome with his hat shoved back and his face flushed from riding. The laughter of his friends made it obvious they'd all had a good time on the ride. A wave of jealousy swept over me. I turned away, swallowing a giant lump in my throat.

I quickly fastened my seat belt. "Let's get out of here, Gram," I urged.

She waved in Troy's direction. I didn't look to see if he'd returned her greeting but I assumed he did. "He's such a nice boy," Gram said, shaking her head. "But stubborn like his father. His mood will wear off in time, dear. You'll see."

I shrugged. "I don't really care." But I did. It hurt to lose a good friend like Troy, especially when it had seemed as if romance had been just around the corner. But I had taken care of that, and now our romance would never happen.

The days continued to run together. I worked in the outside ring when the weather was good and Troy was busy with students inside. When he worked outside, I worked inside with the other riders. Whenever I managed to have a few minutes alone I practiced simple dressage with Gingersnap. She responded well, picking up the steps like a pro. I think her rhythm was better than mine. During one of my sessions I glanced at the viewing booth and saw Troy leaning against the doorway watching me. I waved, hoping by now he

131

would have thawed a bit. He nodded slightly, then went back outside. Troy was really being unreasonable, I thought. How long would he go on ignoring me? Forfeiting the competition wasn't *that* terrible a deed. And I had done it to make him happy. Why didn't he see that?

I was glad when Lorie phoned that night. "Get your best bikini out of mothballs!" she exclaimed. "I'm having a pool party Sunday."

"Sounds great," I told her. "I need a change of scenery."

"Well, don't worry," she replied. "I have the day off work and I am planning to *celebrate!* Good time guaranteed for Sunday, so be there."

"I will, I will," I said, and promised I'd come over a little early to help with any setups. When I hung up the phone, I was smiling— something I hadn't done in what seemed like a long time.

I actually felt cheerful on Sunday as I put on my new blue bikini and beach jacket. It was a beautiful day with the sun shining bright and hot. When Gram dropped me off at Lorie's house, I ran around to the back, where she'd said the party would be.

The blue-green pool looked so inviting, and on a table Lorie had already laid out lots of sandwiches and a big cooler of soda. I just helped her open some bags of chips and pretzels and other snacks. The kids started to arrive soon after I did. Margaret and Jimmy Townes came together. And Janet sauntered into the backyard, wearing a fiery red string bikini. She hung onto Nick Willis's arm as if she was afraid he'd get away. I wondered who else was coming.

When I asked Lorie, she looked at the four clowning in the pool, and shrugged. "Not many. I thought I'd keep the party small. Joe should be here soon."

I dove off the diving board and swam the length of the pool, feeling refreshed and exhilarated, but when I pulled myself out of the water the first person I saw was Troy. He stood at the edge of the pool talking with Lorie and Joe. Lorie glanced at me, giving me a big wink. Then I knew. She had arranged the party to get Troy and me back on speaking terms. I shook my head and slipped back into the water to swim to the other end of the pool. I wished with all my heart that Lorie's plan would work. But I had the feeling that once Troy saw me, he would leave.

I heard three splashes and knew that Troy had joined Lorie and Joe in the pool. Then someone started a game of ringball—a pool version of basketball. I knew I couldn't hover at the shallow end of the pool like a child forever. So, I took a deep breath and joined in. After all, I wasn't the one who was acting unreasonable. If Troy didn't like my being there, that was his problem. He must have known I'd be at any party of Lorie's anyway.

When he saw me at first, Troy glared at me, but kept his poise. He even seemed to put aside our disagreement as we all laughed and splashed, trying to get a basket. He tossed the ball toward the floating ring. It missed and bounced off the top of my head. It happened so fast I was momentarilly stunned. Could it be he was trying to get my attention? I took a deep breath, doubled over and let myself sink to the bottom of the pool. In seconds strong arms encircled my waist from behind and pulled me to the surface. "Are you okay, Ronnie?" Troy's voice sounded concerned.

I shook my head to clear the water from my eyes. "Oh!" I exclaimed. "Hi, Troy. No need for concern. I'm fine. It was only a beach ball. And I have a hard head."

Troy scowled at me. "Nice joke, Ronnie." I could hear the others continuing with the game. "Another dirty trick," he exclaimed angrily, diving beneath the water. He swam over to join the group in the middle of the pool. I had done it again. If Troy was about to make up with me, I had spoiled it. There would be no reconciliation at Lorie's pool party.

The game had lost its appeal. I pulled myself out of the water, spread a towel on the deck, and stretched out to sun myself. The game continued, noisier than ever. I had an idea Troy was putting on an act for my benefit, and he seemed to be enjoying every second. When Lorie joined me a few minutes later she shook her head at me.

"That was a dumb thing to do, you know. I think Troy was about to forget he was angry with you. Now he's seething. He figures you made him look stupid, diving after you like that." She spread a towel and stretched out beside me. "I thought this pool bash might get you two back together, but I don't think it's going to work.

I sat up, adjusting my sunglasses. "Who cares? There are other guys in the world. Maybe I'll just look around and see if I can find another place to board Gingersnap. That way I won't have to run into Troy Bennett every day." I shrugged as though I didn't care, but I could feel tears stinging my eyes. I pretended it was water from my dripping hair and blotted my face and head with a towel.

When the game ended the others came out of the pool, and we sat around eating sandwiches and drinking ice-cold soda. Then Lorie turned on her stereo radio and she and Joe decided to dance. Quickly, Margaret and Jimmy, then Nick and Janet followed suit. I watched from my position on the deck, while

Troy sat casually on the diving board sipping his drink. The three couples danced to several popular tunes, but then Lorie snapped off the radio abruptly when a commercial came on.

"Hey," Margaret protested. "We were just getting started."

"I know," Lorie said. "I'll turn it on later if anyone wants to dance."

"Sure we do." Janet hugged her thin red beach jacket around herself, shivering. "It keeps me warm."

"You're always cold," Lorie told her. "Look, gang, I've got a brilliant idea. I told Joe and he agrees. Now listen up. We all know there's a dumb feud going on here with certain people who shall remain nameless. It has to do with a blue ribbon, just a shiny piece of cloth, right?"

Heads nodded, including mine. What was Lorie up to now? "So . . . . why don't we put our clever heads together and try to come up with a solution to this problem." Her arm made a sweeping movement to include Troy and myself.

"Good idea, Lorie," Margaret agreed. "Who has an idea?"

"Why don't these two just shake hands and start over?" Joe suggested.

Troy's eyes met mine and we both looked away.

"Not such a good idea, I guess," Jimmy said.

"They could flip a coin to see who will apologize," Janet offered.

Troy glared at her. "Ronnie's the one who threw the show. I'm not apologizing for anything."

I squared my shoulders. "Well neither am I. At the time I thought I did the right thing. I really wanted that blue ribbon. I only gave it up so you could win for your father."

Groaning, Lorie opened another can of soda. "This is getting us nowhere. . . fast."

We all sat sipping soda in silence. Then suddenly an idea hit me. But would Troy go for it? "Why don't we have a rematch—a race. It's not the same as a show, but this way we don't need a judge. We both own fast quarter horses, so what could be better? Winner takes the blue ribbon. What do you think?"

"I like it." Janet nodded emphatically.

"Great idea," Nick agreed.

"Very fair." Margaret smiled in my direction.

Jimmy shrugged. "It might solve things."

Lorie stood in front of me. "I think for once you're making sense."

All eyes went to Troy. He got to his feet and walked around the deck, obviously thinking about my idea. I knew that Troy was good at keeping his true feelings hidden when he wanted to. Now, he showed no reaction at all to my suggestion. Joe went over to stand in front of him, reaching out to shake his shoulders.

"Come on, man, how about a race?"

Troy took a deep breath. "Sure . . . why not? We'll have a flag race."

He didn't look too pleased about it, but he was outnumbered.

"Let's do it tomorrow," I suggested. "The sooner the better." I wanted to race before I changed my mind.

Troy nodded. "That's the way I feel. Be at the Double B in the morning at nine."

"Make it at night so we can all be there," Lorie said. "Some of us work during the day."

Troy shook his head. His eyes met mine. "This race is between Ronnie and me. We'll do it alone."

"Fair enough," I agreed. I felt better than I had in weeks. Tomorrow Troy and I would ride in the most important race of our lives. I had to admit my plan was brilliant. If it worked.

Chapter Thirteen

I couldn't get to sleep that night. Jumbled thoughts were spinning around and around in my head. When I'd first blurted out the idea for the race between Troy and me I thought it was a brilliant suggestion. I only wished I had come up with it sooner. If it worked and solved things between Troy and me it would be great. If it didn't? I kept seeing the look on Troy's face when I urged Gingersnap to go lame. I would never forget his expression of anger and resentment. If only I had known how he would react. I'd thought I was doing him a favor, helping him out with his dad. I tossed and turned a while longer before I finally fell asleep.

When I woke up the sky was bright. Mom and Dad were at work and Gram was getting ready to do a few hours of private-duty nursing in town. She poked her head in my room.

"Hello, sleepy head. I was just going to wake

you. If you hurry and get dressed I'll drop you off at the Double B on my way to work."

I nodded sleepily. "Thanks, Gram. I'll be down in ten minutes."

I took a quick shower before changing into my lucky jeans. Then I picked out my bright blue T-shirt with the slogan BLUE IS FOR WINNERS written across the front. I had a few things to prove to Troy today, and I wanted him to know it. First, I was going to win our race. And second, I was going to win back Troy's friendship.

I stood at my dresser, dabbing on a touch of pink lipstick. No harm in trying to look good. I smiled sweetly at my reflection. Just maybe Troy would notice. I brushed my hair, whirled around once for a final inspection in the mirror, and headed for the stairs.

Gram had toast and juice ready for me and joined me at the table. "I'm not sure I can eat," I told her. "This is an important race today, Gram. It could make things right again for Troy and me."

Gram brushed toast crumbs off the front of her white uniform. "I think it's best that the race is just for you and Troy, without any onlookers."

I nodded, nibbling at a piece of toast. "It's kind of a personal thing, you know?"

Gram smiled. "I hope it turns out well, Ronnie."

We left for the farm a few minutes later. I felt more uptight than I had before competing at the horse shows.

When we arrived at the stables Troy was waiting at the corral. I watched Gram leave, then joined him at the fence. "Hi," I said quietly. He looked sleepy, as if he hadn't been up very long. My heartbeat speeded up just being near him. I tried a smile. "Are you ready for this?"

He shrugged, looking indifferent. "Why not. It sounds fair. What do you say we get it over with?"

I sighed. It would be nice if he showed a bit of enthusiasm. My legs suddenly felt like rubber. The moment of truth was at hand. There was no backing out of the race.

We headed for the barn. Troy's blue ribbon hung over Arrow's stall. He took it down and crammed it into his back pocket. We worked in silence as we saddled our horses for the race. I glanced over Gingersnap's back at Troy, wondering if he felt as nervous as I did. Finally, we led Gingersnap and Arrow out into the sunny barnyard and mounted. My confidence returned as we rode into the field next to the barn where Troy had already set up the two barrels ready for the flag race.

Troy reined Arrow in next to the first barrel. A yellow and blue flag was stuck in a bucket of sand on top of the barrel. "If it's okay with you," he began, "whoever rides first will take the flag from this bucket, race down the field and put the flag in the bucket on the second barrel. The next rider will race down and bring it back here. I'll handle the stopwatch for you and you can do the same for me. How does that sound?"

I felt exhilarated. The breeze tugged at my hair and cooled my cheeks. I took a long, deep breath. I was ready to go and so was Gingersnap. "Sounds fine to me. I think I should warn you, Troy, I plan to win this race."

I thought I detected a slight smile cross his face as he glanced at the logo of my T-shirt. "Good. Me too."

Well, it was a short conversation, but at least we were speaking again. I looked across the field to the second barrel. It was such a short run, but so important. The race could restore our friendship, or end it forever. I shivered at the thought.

Troy pulled the blue ribbon from his back pocket and put it on top of the barrel. The sun glistened off the shiny material.

"Why don't we flip a coin to see who runs first?" I suggested. "I drop the coins when I try, so you flip. I'll take heads." I reached into my pocket and came up empty-handed. "I hope you have a quarter."

Troy pulled a coin out of the pocket of his jeans. "We're in luck. Here goes. . ." He flipped the coin in the air and caught it, slapping it on the back of his other hand. "Will you look at that," he exclaimed. "Tails."

"Fine," I said, unconcerned. He may have won the toss, but I was determined that he wouldn't win the race.

Troy handed me the stopwatch and moved his horse into place next to the barrel. The breeze stirred the flag in the bucket. "I'll start you out," I told him. "Ready?" I heard Arrow snort. "Get set. . . go!"

I started the stopwatch as Arrow lunged into action. In a flash, Troy had snatched the flag from the bucket. The horse's hooves kicked up dirt in the wild dash for the second barrel. Troy plunged the flag into the bucket and Arrow headed back toward Gingersnap and me.

When Troy reined in beside the barrel, I stopped the watch. "Not bad." I handed him the watch so he could see his time. "Not bad" had been an understatement. Troy and Arrow were a super team. My confidence wavered. Winning this race would not be easy. I leaned forward to whisper in Gingersnap's ear. "You have to run like the wind, girl.

We'll soon know who really takes the blue ribbon."

Gingersnap moved into place. Troy gave me the signal. . . and we were off. I urged Gingersnap forward at full speed. My heart pounded to the beat of her clattering hooves and the field was a blur as we raced toward the barrel at the far end. I reached out my hand and grabbed the flag, at the same time guiding Ginger around the barrel and back toward Troy. Again I reached out my hand, this time to stick the flag into the bucket of sand.

When Gingersnap skidded to a stop next to Troy he waved the stopwatch in the air. "You're not going to believe this!"

I couldn't tell from his expression if he was angry or pleased. "Don't keep me in suspense," I said panting. "Which one of us hangs the blue ribbon on the wall?"

Troy leaned forward in his saddle, handing me the stopwatch. "See for yourself."

I looked at the watch, then at Troy. He smiled at me. The smile eased into a wide grin, then a real laugh.

I joined in. "Unbelievable!" I exclaimed, shaking my head. "Now what do we do?"

Troy shrugged. "Maybe it's fate. This could settle everything if we let it."

"How?" I gave him a questioning look. "We

ran the race in the same time, so nothing is settled. We still don't know who takes the blue ribbon. It seems to me we have two choices. We can either run the race again, or tear the ribbon in half," I said.

Actually, the ribbon no longer mattered to me. The race had been fair, and we were both winners. But I wasn't sure how Troy felt about it.

Troy eased Arrow so close our legs touched. "This calls for a brief deliberation," he said, dismounting. "Let's sit down and talk it over."

I dismounted and we led the horses over to a log used as a practice trail-ride jump. We sat down, letting the horses graze on the field grass. I waited to hear what Troy would say next.

He turned to look at me, his expression serious. "I've seen judges have a tough time making a decision sometimes. Let's put ourselves in their place if they had to call a win on this one. What do you think?"

I took a deep breath, watching the horses munch the lush grass. "Well, you and Arrow were good—great, even. I'd say it was a perfect run." I looked at Troy. "How did you see it?"

He reached out and idly plucked a wildflower from the long grasses. "I think you and Gingersnap should get a top score. You did a terrific job."

"So we still have a major problem. And a lot depends on the outcome of this race, you know," I said, glancing at him cautiously.

He nodded. "Can I be the deciding judge?"

Since the outcome didn't matter to me anymore, I shrugged. "Sure."

He cleared his throat. "We the judges have arrived at a decision after a long and difficult deliberation. We both won. There's no way to change that unless we run another race. That seems stupid since it could happen again— we're just too evenly matched. So . . ." He squared his shoulders. "We the judges think the blue ribbon should be shared until the same show next year."

I had to bite my lip to keep from laughing with joy. "Then we can compete again. To be fair, we the judges think Troy should take the ribbon first, keep it for a month," I said with mock seriousness, "then hand it over to his competitor who will keep it for a month, then return it, and so on. How does that sound to you?" I looked at Troy. I could see the old smile in his eyes. I may have only tied the race, but I'd won back his friendship and that was worth far more than a dumb old ribbon.

"Sounds good to me," he said quietly. "We

did a great job solving our dilemma. It's too bad we didn't settle it a long time ago. I've missed you, Ronnie. I guess I overreacted, and I'm sorry." He took my hand in his and squeezed it.

"And I'm sorry I forfeited the Bronson show," I said. "That was a big mistake. But I was only trying to—"

"I know." Troy glanced my way. "Hey! Running that race made me hungry. How about going to the Burger Barn?" His eyes searched my face. "If you want to be seen with me, that is."

My spirits soared. Did I *want* to? "Sure!" I replied.

We walked the horses back to the barnyard, unsaddled them, and rubbed them down. We did our tasks slowly, each working silently. But it wasn't a strained silence. It was as if we both had a lot of thinking to do.

Finally, I broke the silence. "You better watch out next year, Troy Bennett," I teased. "I'll show you no mercy."

He led Arrow into the barn, turning him into his stall. Troy looked very serious. I had a sinking feeling. Had I said the wrong thing again?

I needn't have worried. When Troy turned back around, he pulled me gently into his arms. His kiss was so sweet and tender, and full of the romance I'd been longing for. "Do you know, I consider myself very lucky, Ronnie," he said softly. "I want to thank you."

I gave him a puzzled look. "For what?" I was still in shock from the hug and kiss.

"For being so special. I hated these past few weeks when we barely said hello to each other. But I was too stubborn to say I was sorry. I know you did what you did for me . . . and for Dad."

He stepped back and looked at me seriously. "You know, it's funny. When I first met you and saw how good you were, I felt threatened. I knew you'd be serious competition, and I knew how important winning is to my dad—" He paused to give me a crooked smile. "Not that I don't like to win, too, but sometimes I get the feeling that Dad is counting on me to do what he can't do anymore. . . . But anyway, when you threw the race, I felt like you didn't think I was good enough to do it on my own—and that made me *mad*!"

I grinned at him. "I'd noticed."

Troy reached over and took my hand, his face turning serious again. "I know now that that was stupid. You did it because you care. You gave up something important to you for me and my dad, and I just threw that in your face. I really was a jerk about it, Ronnie, and it's high time I thanked you. It's a little late, but thanks—you're terrific."

"I'll agree with you on that, son." Mr. Bennett wheeled out of the small barn and smiled up at me. "I knew what you did, young lady. I saw you put Gingersnap through her tricks one day in the ring, so I know she's trained to go lame. You sacrificed a lot for Troy and me, and you made me do some serious thinking."

He looked up at Troy, who was staring at him, dumbfounded. "From now on, I want you to ride for yourself. Ride because you love being in the saddle. If you win, great. If you don't . . . " Mr. Bennett shrugged. "I know I've been putting a lot of pressure on you lately. I have to admit, it's tough knowing I can't do something I love as much as riding anymore. But I can't expect you to live my life for me—that's not fair to you. Just do your best, son, that's all I've ever really wanted from you. Blue is a pretty color, but so is red, and green, and yellow. I'm proud of *you* . . . win *or* lose." He smiled at Troy, then winked at me. Without another word, he wheeled himself toward the house.

Troy stared after his father for a moment, then turned to me with a look of disbelief. "Did I hear what I think I heard?" he asked me, shaking his head.

I nodded. "I heard it too. And I'm really glad."

At that moment, Gingersnap nudged me in the back, causing me to lose my balance and stumble toward Troy. He reached out to grab me before I banged into the fence. We were very close. His beautiful brown eyes stared into mine for a minute and I felt myself melt. When he leaned down to kiss me for the second time I wasn't surprised. But I was very, very happy.

SWEET DREAMS are fresh, fun and exciting—alive with the flavor of the contemporary teen scene—the joy and doubt of first love. If you've missed any SWEET DREAMS titles, then you're missing out on your kind of stories, written about people like you!

☐ 26789 PAST PERFECT #134 Fran Michaels $2.50
☐ 26902 GEARED FOR ROMANCE #135 $2.50
  Shan Finney
☐ 26903 STAND BY FOR LOVE #136 $2.50
  Carol MacBain
☐ 26948 ROCKY ROMANCE #137 $2.50
  Sharon Dennis Wyeth
☐ 26949 HEART & SOUL #138 Janice Boies $2.50
☐ 27005 THE RIGHT COMBINATION #139 $2.50
  Jannah Beecham
☐ 27061 LOVE DETOUR #140 Stefanie Curtis $2.50
☐ 27062 WINTER DREAMS #141 Barbara Conklin $2.50
☐ 27124 LIFEGUARD SUMMER #142 Jill Jarnow $2.50
☐ 27125 CRAZY FOR YOU #143 Jahnna Beecham $2.50
☐ 27174 PRICELESS LOVE #144 Laurie Lykken $2.50
☐ 27175 THIS TIME FOR REAL #145 $2.50
  Susan Gorman
☐ 27228 GIFTS FROM THE HEART #146 $2.50
  Joanne Simbal
☐ 27229 TRUST IN LOVE #147 Shan Finney $2.50
☐ 27275 RIDDLES OF LOVE #148 Judy Baer $2.50
☐ 27276 PRACTICE MAKES PERFECT #149 $2.50
  Jahnna Beecham
☐ 27357 SUMMER SECRETS #150 Susan Blake $2.50
☐ 27358 FORTUNES OF LOVE #151 Mary Schultz $2.50
☐ 27413 CROSS-COUNTRY MATCH #152 $2.50
  Ann Richards
☐ 27475 THE PERFECT CATCH #153 $2.50
  Laurie Lykken

Prices and availability subject to change without notice.

— —

BANTAM
SHOP·AT·HOME
C·A·T·A·L·O·G

Special Offer
Buy a Bantam Book
for only 50¢.

Now you can order the exciting books you've been wanting to read straight from Bantam's latest catalog of hundreds of titles. *And* this special offer gives you the opportunity to purchase a Bantam book for only 50¢. Here's how:

By ordering any five books at the regular price per order, you can also choose any other single book listed (up to a $5.95 value) for only 50¢. Some restrictions do apply, so for further details send for Bantam's catalog of titles today.

Just send us your name and address and we'll send you Bantam Book's SHOP AT HOME CATALOG!

EXCITING NEWS FOR ROMANCE READERS

Loveletters—the all new, hot-off-the-press Romance Newsletter. Now you can be the first to know:

What's Coming Up:
* Exciting offers
* New romance series on the way

What's Going Down:
* The latest gossip about the SWEET VALLEY HIGH gang
* Who's in love . . . and who's not
* What Loveletters fans are saying.

Who's New:
* Be on the inside track for upcoming titles

If you don't already receive Loveletters, fill out this coupon, mail it in, and you will receive Loveletters several times a year. Loveletters . . . you're going to love it!

Please send me my free copy of Loveletters

Name _____ Date of Birth _____

Address _____

City _____ State _____ Zip _____

To: LOVELETTERS
   BANTAM BOOKS
   PO BOX 1005
   SOUTH HOLLAND, IL 60473